Double Spell

Double Spell

JANET LUNN

Tundra Books

Copyright © 1968, 2003 by Janet Lunn

First published in Canada by Peter Martin Associates, 1968
First published in the United States as *Twin Spell* by Harper and Row, 1968
First published in this edition by Tundra Books, Toronto, 2003

Published in Canada by Tundra Books,
481 University Avenue, Toronto, Ontario M5G 2E9

Published in the United States by Tundra Books of Northern New York,
P.O. Box 1030, Plattsburgh, New York 12901

Library of Congress Control Number: 2003100906

National Library of Canada Cataloguing in Publication

Lunn, Janet, 1928-
Double spell / Janet Lunn.

ISBN 0-88776-660-9

I. Title.

PS8573.U55D6 2003   jC813'.54   C2003-900694-8
                       PZ7

We acknowledge the financial support of the Government of Canada
through the Book Publishing Industry Development Program and that
of the Government of Ontario through the Ontario Media Development
Corporation's Ontario Book Initiative. We further acknowledge the support
of the Canada Council for the Arts and the Ontario Arts Council for
our publishing program.

Design: Cindy Elisabeth Reichle
Printed and bound in Canada

1 2 3 4 5 6   08 07 06 05 04 03

To the twins,
Sanda and Judith,
and their five friends,
Eric, Alec, Jeffrey,
Kate, and John

Contents

I

The Doll

The twins found the doll on a cold wet Saturday in early spring. They found it in an antique shop, which was odd because neither Jane nor Elizabeth had ever thought of going into an antique shop before. At age twelve, they didn't think much about dolls anymore, either. And yet, on this rainy Saturday morning, they did both.

They were hurrying up Yonge Street, already late home, not paying much attention to anyone or anything they passed, when suddenly they stopped. Both at once, as though they'd been jerked by an invisible cord. They turned, splashed across the sidewalk, and stared into the window of a little shop. ANTIQUES, DOLLS MENDED, it said in scratched gold letters across its front. In the window there were old books, bits of tarnished jewelry, china dolls' heads, old cups – and the little wooden doll.

The doll was about seven inches high, with arms that stuck straight out from its sides. Its clothes were a dress and bonnet of a bygone time, tattered and faded to a soft pink-brown color. Its feet were a pair of black velvet boots with most of the velvet gone. The paint was worn from its face and chipped in spots. Except for its eyes, which were still a deep and shining blue, the doll was a neglected and forlorn little thing. Not a beauty in any way.

What was it about the doll? Jammed between a dusty green glass bowl and a broken clock, it was hard to see. But the twins had seen it, it had stopped them, pulled them, and held them spellbound.

For quite a while, they stood and stared. People bumped past. Rain drizzled uncomfortably down the necks of their yellow slickers and into the tops of their boots. Still they stood.

"Let's go look," Elizabeth said finally, walking toward the shop entrance.

"We promised to go home and baby-sit William," Jane remembered.

"We only need to stay a minute." Elizabeth's foot was already on the doorstep.

Usually it was sensible Jane who prevailed but this time, probably because she wanted to so badly, she followed her sister.

Inside, the shop was dark and dusty but warm. All the twins could see at first were vague shapes that turned out, in a minute or two, to be high-backed chairs, bedsteads, tables, and more of the things that cluttered the window.

From somewhere at the back, a woman appeared – "sort of like a fairy godmother right up out of nowhere," Elizabeth said later when she was telling William about it. She was little and old like the doll and seemed to belong to the shop. "How do you do," she said, and Elizabeth was encouraged by her warm smile.

"We . . . we'd like to see the little doll please," she stammered. Elizabeth didn't usually stammer. She felt strange and nervous.

"Which doll is it?" asked the woman. "We have quite a few as you can see."

And, now they could see, the twins noticed that one whole long wall was covered with shelves full of dolls.

Jane took charge. "It's the one in the window. That one." She walked over and pointed to the straight back of the window doll.

"Oh," the woman sounded regretful, "I'm afraid that one isn't for sale. It's quite old, you see. I use it just for show."

Elizabeth felt she had to hold the doll, if only once. "Could we look at it in here, just for a minute," she pleaded.

"I don't see why not." The twins watched breathlessly as the woman reached into the window case, lifted the doll out, and put it carefully into the two pairs of hands stretched out.

Their fingers touched the face gently, straightened the bonnet on its head, smoothed the old shawl. It was not a battered antique doll they held, not at this moment. It was a familiar loved thing, long lost, almost forgotten.

The feeling was gone almost at once, faded, but leaving behind, like a trailing cloud, a slight sense of somewhere else.

With a great sigh Elizabeth handed it to the shop woman. The woman took it, but didn't move to put it back in the window. She held it, looked at it as though she were trying to make up her mind.

"How much money have you got?" she asked.

The twins poked hands into their pockets and pulled out two dollars and fifty-three cents all told.

"That'll do," the woman said. "I'll get the box." She was gone and back before they quite realized what she was doing.

The box was as old-looking as the doll. It was leather, just big enough to hold the doll. The leather had peeled off in many spots. More of it rubbed off as the shop woman held it. Its color was faded like the doll's dress to that same pink-brown shade. It was decorated with studs around its edges and had an elaborately worked catch.

With great care the woman wrapped the doll in a piece of blue cloth from the box, laid it inside, and closed the lid.

"I don't know why I'm doing this," she scolded herself. "I should have my head read, I really should, but the doll seems to belong to you. I'd never feel right about keeping it now, I wouldn't. You take care of it. You take care of it." She thrust the box into Elizabeth's hands.

The twins were too bewildered by what had happened to them and too surprised by this sudden gift to say anything. At last Jane remembered her manners.

"Thank you. Thank you very much. We will." She started toward the door.

"Yes," said Elizabeth vaguely. It was all she could think of to say. "Yes," she said again, and trotted after her sister.

2

Aunt Alice

It was raining harder now. A few people scurried past, their heads, like turtles', pulled closely into their collars. The wind was high and cold. Jane and Elizabeth stood close together outside the Antiques, Dolls Mended shop.

Whatever spell the little wooden doll had cast over them was gone. Jane shivered and pulled her slicker tight up against her neck.

"Wasn't that the funniest thing?"

"Maybe it's a mystery," Elizabeth found this sudden idea very exciting. "Maybe this doll has some kind of magic or something – something that will lead us to a great discovery." She shoved the leather box more snugly and securely under her arm.

"Oh honestly! You and your mysteries and magics!" Jane said disgustedly. "Just because we saw an old doll and liked it especially does it have to be a mystery?"

6

"Well, you have to admit it was sort of odd both of us seeing it at the same time like that – and anyway," Elizabeth remembered, "you said it yourself. You said, wasn't it fun . . ."

"Oh, let's not argue. Where'll we go?"

Elizabeth understood. Jane meant someplace special, someplace just exactly right to take the doll. The twins were like that. They often understood each other with half the number of words it takes most people.

"Aunt Alice," she answered promptly. Neither she nor Jane remembered their promise to go straight home to take care of six-year-old William. Almost before the words were out of Elizabeth's mouth, Jane was poking through her pockets for streetcar tickets to take them to Aunt Alice's.

Aunt Alice wasn't really their aunt. She was their mother's aunt, whom they had met for the first time only a few weeks earlier. When the Hubbard family had moved from the country to Spring View Acres in the suburbs of Toronto, Aunt Alice was still in England where she had been living for years. Just last month she had come home to live in her big old house near the lake. Straightaway she had come to visit the Hubbard family. They had decided then and there that Aunt Alice was just the aunt they'd always wanted ("instant aunt," the twins' thirteen-year-old brother, Joe, called her. And Pat, their older brother, had agreed she was a great improvement over Aunt Marvel, who "always gave you behavior talks").

Aunt Alice was certainly the right person to take an antique doll to show.

Suddenly Elizabeth remembered, "We don't know where she lives."

"Yes we do," crowed Jane, "or anyway, I do. Aunt Alice told me we should come down to the beach and go swimming when the warm weather comes and I asked her for directions."

"Do you have them here?"

"Yep. I put them in my purse so I'd have them – just in case."

Elizabeth was dumbfounded. She could never get over the way Jane always made everything work out. "Oh, you and your organizing," she complained but, nevertheless, she was delighted to see her sister produce Aunt Alice's address – Alice Armitage, Number Five, Sabiston Court – complete with directions telling how to get there.

With no trouble at all they took the subway and the long streetcar ride to the east end of the city where Aunt Alice lived, Jane leading the way and giving directions, Elizabeth following. They felt as though they were off on an adventure.

Not once did they remember their promise to their mother. Mama, William, Spring View Acres – it was all far away. When they got off the streetcar where the directions said they should – Hayberry Street – it looked to the twins like another land. The old streets, so many tall trees, the big houses, some tall, some wide, were so different from the broad streets without sidewalks and rows of small modern houses in Spring View Acres. And there was the lake right down at the end of Hayberry Street, rising and falling in giant mounds under the wind, gray-green and cold in the rain. They could smell it from the top of the street, a wonderful fresh, exciting smell.

Sabiston Court, where Aunt Alice lived, was a tiny street that curled away from Hayberry Street three quarters of the way down. Number Five was on the corner, its back to the lake. It was a tall house, three storeys, and quite wide. There was a two storey porch all across the front and a high eight-sided tower at its left-hand corner.

The house looked enormous and unfriendly. The dark sky hung over it. The lake loomed behind. The rain poured heavily all around it.

Jane began to hold back. "Do you think we should?" she asked nervously, "after all, Aunt Alice didn't invite us."

Elizabeth wasn't so sure any more either, but she wasn't going to let Jane know that. "Are you scared?" she asked.

"No." Jane marched up to the front door, lifted the heavy iron knocker, and pounded it hard.

They waited a nervous moment or two. The door opened and there was Aunt Alice.

"Well," she said, "you've come for tea."

"We were uptown and we just thought maybe you'd like to see us," said Elizabeth carelessly, as though she often dropped in on people who lived at the other end of the city. "We've brought something to show you."

"Good," said Aunt Alice. "Come in. Or do you want tea in the rain?"

The twins giggled and felt better even as they dripped rainwater all over Aunt Alice's front hall carpet.

Inside, the house wasn't nearly as forbidding as out. It was quite inviting. After they had taken off their raincoats and boots in the wide front hall, Aunt Alice led them through into her little sitting room at the back. From the window the twins could see the lake heaving in the storm, but inside there was a fire in the red brick fireplace. The walls of the sitting room had red and yellow flowered paper, which made it even cozier, and a deep red couch along one side of the fireplace. On the other side was an old high-backed rocker (*just like the one in the Dolls Mended shop*, thought Elizabeth) that had Aunt Alice's book lying face down on it. The twins noticed it there and politely sat, side-by-side, on the couch.

Aunt Alice was as good as they remembered. There were no tiresome questions about being out on a day like this, how colds are caught, or anything. She did tell them how much they looked alike, but in such a way that it was funnier than it was uncomfortable, picking them apart (they decided later) as though they were verbs and nouns and things.

"Uncle Oliver's small ears," she murmured. "Marvel's chestnut hair and fair skin. Armitage nose and mouth." She put her hand up to her own long thin nose and rather wide mouth. "No sign of the Cunningham black hair or eyes, that's . . ."

"That's what Joe is," interrupted Elizabeth. Joe was a trial and torment to them both. "Miserable black eyes," she added, "and he has a long nose too."

"Always poking it into other people's business," muttered Jane.

"Pat has hair like ours," Elizabeth continued. Pat was their fifteen-year-old brother. "But William has golden hair." She sighed enviously. "Mama says he looks like her grandmother."

"Yes," said Aunt Alice, "Mother had golden hair." She smiled. "But not freckles. Must get those from your father. Didn't have those eyes either." Aunt Alice examined them carefully, as though she were memorizing them. "No," she said, "never seen eyes that shape – beech leaves." She smiled again. "Your turn now."

The twins looked at her, surprised.

"Come," said Aunt Alice. "What do you say? Tall, skinny, ski nose, ski face, wrinkles, faded blue eyes – and a blob of cotton on top."

The twins couldn't help laughing. Aunt Alice's description of herself wasn't that wrong. Her face was long and thin (and her nose), although maybe not as thin as a ski, and it had a blob of white cotton on top. *No, not a blob,* thought Elizabeth, *more like a cream puff – nice.* Her face had wrinkles, lots of them, but they were good wrinkles that looked like fun. And Aunt Alice's eyes were bright blue like the doll's, not faded.

Embarrassed by all this close inspection of each other, Jane changed the subject. "I like your house," she said.

"Yes," Aunt Alice agreed, "good house. Always been my house. Grew up here. So did your grandmother and Uncle

Arthur. Family always lived here. Good place to live."

She paused. "Better for you than me," she added. Elizabeth thought of the tight-packed little bungalow in Spring View Acres and sighed. She thought of the walk-in cupboard she and Jane shared as a bedroom in the little house and sighed again.

"It's beautiful," said Jane.

"Well then," Aunt Alice said, leaning forward in her chair, "show me what you've brought. Then look around my house. Then tea. How's that?"

The twins thought it a fine plan. Elizabeth took the box she had been hugging tightly all the way from the Antiques, Dolls Mended shop and set it on her lap, lifted the lid, and brought out the little doll. In the comfortable surroundings of Aunt Alice's old house, the doll seemed quite at home. Elizabeth smoothed the faded cloth of its dress lovingly. "It's called Amelia," she said, handing it to Aunt Alice.

"Isn't that funny," said Jane, "that's the name I was thinking."

Aunt Alice looked from Jane to Elizabeth. "Twins. Happen often?"

"I guess so," said Jane. Elizabeth said nothing. They both hated twin questions.

Aunt Alice didn't notice. She was already busy inspecting the doll.

"It's old. Don't really know about dolls, toys, and things. Can tell it's old though. Might be valuable. Interesting to find out. Good face even with the broken nose." She smiled and handed the doll back to Elizabeth.

Elizabeth sat looking at its carved arms and legs while Aunt Alice talked in her short quick sentences about fixing it up and restoring it to its original state. She could picture it as clearly as though she had seen it new, in a bright red wool dress with a tiny white shawl, its bonnet fresh and new and its velvet boots soft and rich. Its face had a cheerful smile painted on it, a little carved nose that turned up at the end, and delicately drawn eyebrows and eyelashes for its bright blue eyes. Aunt Alice's voice saying, "Come along, show you your grandmother's house," cut off the vision of Amelia, new and shiny. Reluctantly Elizabeth put the doll back into the box, but she carried the box with her when she got up.

It was a wonderful house – but funny. It looked as though it had been put together not all at one time but like a house a small child makes out of blocks, adding pieces on here and there just because she likes their shapes. The back of the house had the little study where the twins and Aunt Alice had been sitting, divided by a small hall from the kitchen beside it. Beyond that there was the dining room – a round room at the bottom of a short tower, invisible from the front, that stuck up at the back. There were steps up from the kitchen to the long hall that led to the front door, with three more steps down on one side to the living room and on the other to a big spare room ("Used to be dining room. Never use it," said Aunt Alice).

Off the living room was another door opening into the first floor of the tall eight-sided tower.

Upstairs the hall was round like the hub of a wheel, and all the rooms attached to the ends of the short hallways that were the wheel's spokes. It seemed to Jane and Elizabeth as though Aunt Alice opened and closed at least fifty doors. There was one hall longer than the rest that ended with three steps down to another little hall, which led either into a small room at the back of the house or down the kitchen stairs.

"Attic," Aunt Alice said, but didn't open its door.

In order to get to the second-storey room of the back tower they had to go down the back stairs, through the kitchen, and into the dining room, where another set of stairs went up to the tower bedroom.

"I could be Rapunzel," Elizabeth whispered ecstatically. Jane hadn't any longing to be Rapunzel but she did love the round room with all its windows and their deep window seats. They could see the lake clearly, the deserted beach, and the garden just below, sodden in the rain. Off to one side there was an old garage.

"Coach house," Aunt Alice explained. "My father kept a horse and carriage."

"Oh, wouldn't that be marvelous." Right away Elizabeth imagined herself in the carriage. She thought of the little doll and its old fashioned dress. She pictured herself in a dress like that. For a moment she could really see it – not the coach house, strangely enough – but an open-fronted shed in the bright sunshine of a spring day, a horse and cart standing outside, herself in a long blue dress just getting in. She leaned forward. The picture was gone, washed away, and she was looking at the old coach house under the rain.

"There's the attic," Aunt Alice was pointing down to the square back of the house where a little roof peak ended just below the level of the tower window.

"Funny attic," Elizabeth said. "It's lower than this tower."

"Older part of the house," Aunt Alice answered. "Haven't been in it for years. Always found it depressing. Odd," she frowned. "Window's open."

Down the stairs, back through the dining room, up the back stairs again, the twins followed Aunt Alice. "Shut the window," she said. "Can't understand it open at all."

"I don't like it," Jane stood in the hall and shivered.

"Unpleasant place. Not the day to go exploring the attic anyway. Cold up here." Aunt Alice shut the door firmly after her.

And down they went again, single file down the curved stairway to the front hall. And that's when Elizabeth had the accident. She was in the lead. She got as far as the niche in the wall where a gas lamp had once stood – just by the deepest curve – when she tripped. Frantically she clutched the doll's box for support and plunged down, over and over and over to the hall below. The leather box flew out of her hands and shot across the floor. Elizabeth lay crumpled at the foot of the stairs. For almost a whole minute all she could think was to reach the box. Then the pain began with such a rush that when Aunt Alice crouched beside her she didn't know who she was.

The rest of the day was a whirling kaleidoscope. With a sharp order to Jane not to budge the twin, Aunt Alice phoned her doctor. Then she phoned Mama. Mama's voice shrilled over the phone, "was going to call the police, phoned all the hospitals, all the neighbors alarmed . . . oh, Aunt Alice . . ." Jane remembered William. Aunt Alice looked dangerous. Dr. Lorne came from up the street and said Elizabeth's leg was broken. Mama and Papa arrived from Spring View Acres. Mama went with Elizabeth and Dr. Lorne to the hospital. Papa took Jane home (without a word all the way) and put her to bed without supper. He went away again to the hospital.

Joe, because he wanted to hear what had happened, brought shredded wheat and a piece of leftover rhubarb pie to the walk-in cupboard. William came too and Patrick, who stood against the door jamb saying nothing. Marble, the cat, came in with William and settled on the bed. Jane looked at Pat and knew how much Mama had worried. Pat was like that. Without saying a word he could make you think more about what you'd done wrong than all Mama and Papa's scolding could do.

Joe wanted to see the doll. He said it was a pretty silly looking thing to cause all that fuss. William said it looked like Jimmy Macdonald the day he couldn't find his dog.

Then Mr. and Mrs. Hubbard came home with Elizabeth. The boys were sent from the room and Elizabeth settled into the lower bunk. There was no scolding that night but it was obvious there was going to be the next day.

When they were alone, Jane hung her head over the edge of the upper bunk and told Elizabeth she thought it was awful having a broken leg.

"All the same," said Elizabeth, "it was a very interesting day." She tightened her hand around the leather box she had brought to bed with her.

Jane said she supposed so.

It was exactly one week later when Mama came into the living room from answering the telephone with a blank look on her face.

"You won't believe it," she said, "but Aunt Alice fell downstairs and broke her hip. She's going to give us her house."

3

Aunt Alice Gets a Sick Basket

It was true. Aunt Alice had fallen down her front stairs, queerly enough, just by the niche where Elizabeth had fallen. It was going to take months for her hip to heal and Aunt Alice had decided the big house was going to be too much for her. Her visit with the twins had made her think quite a bit about her own childhood in the big house. After that it hadn't taken long for her to make up her mind to move out and invite the Hubbards to move in.

Just like that, they were going to move. One day crammed into the little bungalow, the next a three storey house with towers.

"No more walk-in cupboard," sighed the twins ecstatically.

"No more trumpet practice in the bathroom," said Joe joyfully.

"No more Vasco da Gama on my shoe," chortled Papa – he said this because once, when Elizabeth had been making a plaster of paris map of explorers on the living room floor, Papa had accidentally stepped in it. Jane had had to help build Henry Hudson up all over again and Papa had sworn for weeks that he still had pieces of Vasco da Gama stuck to his shoe.

The new house, or rather Aunt Alice's old house, had room enough for ten social studies projects to be going on at once; room enough for Joe to practice his trumpet in the attic – and no one bothered but the gulls. There would be dinner in the round dining room with its big windows, and no elbows in each other's soup. Best of all as far as the twins were concerned, there would be the big tower bedroom where they would actually have to get out of bed to open not one tiny round window, but great tall windows all around the room. There was no question about the tower room being theirs – a tower for two Rapunzels, Papa called it.

Certainly it was going to be wonderful. The night after Aunt Alice phoned, Mr. and Mrs. Hubbard went to the hospital to visit and (at Aunt Alice's insistence) to arrange the business. The children sat in the living room planning and talking. Jane made cocoa in the kitchen.

"I'm going to be like a princess in the tower," said Elizabeth dreamily, "looking far out to the sea, waiting for . . ."

"You look like some princess," said Joe disgustedly, eyeing her old plaid dressing gown and her leg, in its big white cast, stretched out on the couch in front of her.

"Shut up." said Elizabeth.

"Anyway, I'm going to have the tower and Willy Wallet's going to come and visit. . . ."

"Willy Wallet?" Elizabeth was too horrified to question Joe's appropriation of her tower. Joe's friend, Willy Wallet, was the scourge of the Hubbard household. Nothing was safe from him – Pat's toads and tadpoles, William's precious cars, the twins' games and, worse, the twins' feelings. "Willy Wallet," cried Elizabeth, trying to rise from the couch, "Willy Wallet is never, ever, going to set foot in Aunt Alice's house. If . . ."

"I'm going to have the Huff's dog and keep him in the coach house," Patrick cut across the budding fight. "They don't like it very much. I'm sure they're going to give it to me."

"I want part of the coach house for arts and crafts," Jane came in from the kitchen with a tray of cocoa. "Oh, isn't it all just great!"

"Oh, no you don't," said Pat vehemently. "Oh good, cocoa. That coach house is all mine – m-i-n-e – and dog's."

"And cat's," said Joe, "and water buffalo's and emu's . . ."

"No water buffaloes. No emus," Patrick began. He stopped. He put down his cocoa mug and looked uncomfortable. "It really seems mean thinking up all these good things when it's all because Aunt Alice broke her hip. It isn't fair somehow."

"Well it's not our fault she fell," said Joe defensively. "Anyhow, she's going to get better and she said she's glad to move out of that old house."

"That's true," said Pat.

"I can just hear her say it," Elizabeth mimicked Aunt Alice's tone, "Tired of that old house. Too big for me. Fits you. You have it. . . ." She giggled and went on in her own voice. "As though it were an old dress or something." Her face changed. "What's in this cocoa?"

"It's furniture polish," William said looking at Jane. "Did you put in furniture polish?"

Jane's face grew red. "No I didn't," she said indignantly, "William you're horrid!"

Everyone sniffed the cocoa. William was right. It had an odor that was very remindful of the living room furniture, only not as nice because it was part cocoa.

"Yes, furniture polish. Good old Jane!" Joe put his mug down on the coffee table.

"It's not." Jane marched out to the kitchen. Then she came hack, her face redder than before. "I thought it was vanilla," she said in a small voice.

Four horrified voices asked, "What was it?"

"Lemon flavoring."

"Never mind," said Pat, soothingly. "It's edible."

"Oh, boy!" said Joe, "you've invented a new thing – lemon cocoa. Let's send some to Aunt Alice."

"Joe," said Patrick, "you're a sap but you have the right idea. We should send something to Aunt Alice."

"Why don't we take her a sick basket," suggested Jane, "the way Mama does, with wine and jelly and things, and a book to read?"

Startled, Elizabeth looked at her sister. She started to say something but Joe interrupted, "Mama never did that."

"Well someone did." Jane was puzzled. "Someone took it to a sick old lady."

"I did," Elizabeth said, sitting up. "I did," she said again, "I took it in a dream with the little doll and Mama, and I think you were there too. . . ." She stopped, tried to remember the dream clearly, couldn't, and went on, "Never mind. What I remember is the cart, an old-fashioned wood thing, and I had a long blue dress and the day was very bright and there was water shining, a brook or something, nearby. . . ."

"But," said Jane, "it was my dream. I remember it and I had the doll and a blue dress on. . . ."

"And the doll's dress was red. . . ." Elizabeth was very excited.

"Twins," said Joe. "Twins! Good grief! Twins!"

"There was a little house," Jane went on, ignoring Joe, "a red brick one with a white peak on the front. . . ."

"Like lace."

"Yes, sort of wood lace, and . . ."

"What's all that got to do with Aunt Alice and the basket thing?" Joe put an exclamation mark after his name, which he had just written on Elizabeth's cast.

Elizabeth said nothing. She couldn't remember ever sharing dreams before.

"It should have pickled meat, and flowers on the handle," Jane said, describing the basket in her (and Elizabeth's) dream.

"Pickled meat on the handle? Great!" Joe leaned back in his chair laughing so hard that he knocked over the lamp standing behind him.

"Great," said Pat, "when Papa sees that lamp."

"Well," said Joe, picking himself and the lamp up from the floor, "nobody has to tell him." He looked at William.

It was a good idea, the basket. While Joe tidied up the lamp and got a new bulb from the kitchen, Pat fetched the family picnic basket from the basement. Then they counted their combined money. It came to $2.26.

"Not very much," Joe said, but everyone else decided it would buy some grapes and apples, and maybe some chocolates besides. Jane went to the kitchen for jelly, but all she could find that wasn't full of toast crumbs was a jar of Marmite, so they put that in. Patrick said they couldn't buy any wine until they were twenty-one years old.

"Mama or Papa could get it," suggested William, but Jane thought it had better be a surprise.

"You know how Mama's always saying how much people appreciate it when it's all your own effort," she said. Everyone agreed she was right. No wine.

"There's white wine vinegar in the cupboard in the kitchen," offered William.

"Not the same thing," said Patrick firmly.

"There's a bottle of lemon juice in the fridge. I saw it there," said Jane.

"Funny you didn't put it in the cocoa," Joe remarked.

"See if I ever make cocoa again." Jane was insulted.

"See if I ever drink it," Joe shot back and the others said quickly, "Go get the lemon juice."

The basket was beginning to fill up nicely. As well as the Marmite and the lemon juice there were a couple of oranges from the refrigerator, a tin of tuna fish, a bottle of cologne Jane had got for Christmas from Aunt Marvel, a package of rye krisp, and the promise of grapes and apples and maybe chocolate from the $2.26.

"Now," said Jane in a tone of satisfaction, "we need a good book."

"How about *101 Ways to Annoy Your Doctor*," suggested Joe, "or *Ten Easy Steps to a Broken Back*?"

"Oh," said Jane, stamping her foot, "do you have to make a joke out of everything?"

"How about a history of Toronto," asked Pat, looking high into the top corner of the bookshelf. Jane bounced angrily up from her chair.

"No," he said, "I mean it. Here's a book way up here called *City on the Lake: Being a Brief History of the City of Toronto, 1793-1861.*" He took it down. It was obviously very old and it looked as though it might once have been blue, although it was a dark gray color now. "By William Sabiston," he said.

"Sabiston," said the twins in unison. "That's the name of Aunt Alice's street. Let's do that one," and into the basket went *City on the Lake* by William Sabiston, along with the Marmite, Aunt Marvel's cologne, and the rest.

"Splendid," said Patrick and picked up the basket to be put away until tomorrow when they could buy the fruit and take the offering to Aunt Alice. There was one more thing, flowers for the handle. The twins remembered the trimming on their spring hats and solved that problem. Joe, who could draw quite well, made a card, and the next afternoon Pat marched the basket, complete with its artificial daisies and its grapes and apples (and there had been enough money for chocolates), to Aunt Alice in the hospital.

Aunt Alice wrote them a note telling them all thank you. She did admit that she had given the Marmite to a nurse (Pat said he could sure understand that) but that the fruit had been delicious, the lemon juice also, and the basket very attractive. She said she hadn't known Uncle William had written a book and was delighted to have it. She had found it so interesting she had lent it to the man across the hall who worked in the museum and was particularly interested in Canadian history.

The children were very pleased with themselves. The days were marching on. Raw, cold early spring was turning into warm, soft late spring. Leaves were opening wide on all the trees. Tulip time came and went. The birds in the trees around Aunt Alice's house were making their nests and the lilac in her garden was in full bloom. The lake had lost its green color and sparkled like a bed of brilliants under the sun. Elizabeth's leg had mended quickly. The cast was off and, although she was instructed not to run, she no longer had to use the crutches.

Moving day was fast approaching. The house was a complete chaos of packing boxes and trunks. Marble prowled unhappily among them night and day. Joe packed everything he owned so he'd be ready on moving day and then had to unpack them at least once a day to find the things he needed. Nobody else could find anything and everyone was getting cross about it. Nobody was as cross as Papa, who grumbled and pawed over and over again through the boxes in the living room looking for something he had lost; muttering about having put it high for safe keeping; complaining that there was a conspiracy to prevent him finishing the paper he was working on.

Finally one morning his temper erupted into the crowded kitchen where the family was standing around eating breakfast.

"My job," he shouted, "my life's work, maybe even life itself, depends on this document and now some malevolent malcontent has spirited it away – why?" He raised his fist in the air and stamped his foot on Marble's tail. The cat screamed.

No one else moved.

"Now, David," said Mrs. Hubbard soothingly.

Giving the cat a dirty look, he thundered, "I can't go one single step further in this paper without that book."

"What is the book, dear?" Mama asked. "Maybe we can all help look for it."

"Look for it?" he shouted. "I've BEEN looking for it for weeks – years, it seems. It was a history of this city," he said in careful tones. "It was the only extant copy known of that book, which was written by your mother's great uncle and about which I am writing what I like to think is an important historical paper."

Five spoons rested on five grapefruit halves. Nobody said a word.

Finally William spoke, "Is it a blue book?"

"I don't know what color it was," Papa said testily. "I only know it was called *City on the Lake: Being a Brief History of Toronto*, by William Sabiston, your great-great-great uncle."

"Oh," said Elizabeth – or maybe it was Jane, or Patrick, or Joe, or William. Five pairs of eyes looked uneasily at each other.

It was Jane who told. She took a deep breath. "I . . . we . . . ," she said, "we know what happened to your book."

"You do?" Papa asked in great surprise.

"We sent it in Aunt Alice's sick basket."

Both parents looked at her in complete bewilderment. The children began to explain in a hodgepodge of words – basket, Aunt Alice, hadn't any wine, Marmite, wasn't any jelly, $2.26 even enough for chocolates, said she really liked the book, hadn't remembered at all Uncle William had written it, lent it to the museum man across the hall. Words filled the little kitchen until the look on Papa's face wilted them all one by one. The kitchen was silent.

With great care Papa said, "You – get – that – book – back – today," and got up and left the house.

"Well," said Mama. She glared at them all and went to phone Aunt Alice.

The book was retrieved from the museum man across the hall in the hospital and back in Papa's hands by nightfall. He was so pleased to see it that he said no more about it. In fact he was in such a good mood that when Patrick came in from delivering his newspapers Papa asked him if the Huffs still wanted to give away their little dog and how big was it. When Patrick described its size as about a foot high, Papa said he guessed it wouldn't get too seriously in the way and that if Pat would promise to care for it completely, he could accept it.

The only other thing that came of Aunt Alice's sick basket concerned the twins alone – and the little doll. A night or so after they had put together the basket, a night or so during which Elizabeth had an exciting thought running wildly around in her head, she spoke to Jane about it. Just before they went to bed while Jane was putting her hair into two neat braids and Elizabeth was spreading hers artistically over her shoulders.

"Remember when we were deciding about the sick basket?" she asked, "And you had my dream?"

"Umhm."

"Don't you think it was funny? I mean don't you think there's something fishy about that?"

"What do you mean fishy? You mean being twins? Yes."

"No, stupid, not being twins. Having the same dream – and twice."

"Why?"

"Well," Elizabeth sat down on the edge of her bed looking over at the doll propped on their tall dresser top. Then she looked back at Jane. "Ever since we've had this doll," she said hesitantly, "we've had funny things happen – the same dreams and knowing things and stuff like that."

"Oh, Elizabeth! Just because we had the same dream. Just what Joe said, twins, remember?" Jane leaned way over the top bunk and thrust her face down next to her sister's.

"Twins," she said, "twins."

"No," Elizabeth said seriously, "it's more than that. There's something really queer about the whole thing. Finding it the way we did and knowing its name and having that dream. And there have been a couple of other things too. I'm sure there have. . . . I mean I'm not sure, but I almost am. I . . ." She stopped, not entirely sure just what she did mean.

"Look," she went on, "sometimes I see things I don't really see. I know I do. Long ago things with long dresses and bonnets and once it was the doll with its dress all new. It's weird, but kind of exciting, too."

"Honestly!" Jane bounced back up on her bed. "Mama's right. You have the wildest imagination in all Canada. Maybe even the world. What do you think the doll is – a witch doll or something?" Jane giggled.

Elizabeth was undaunted. "No, I don't. But I think there's something about it. Something more than just us being twins and having the same dreams. They were pretty funny dreams for just one of us to have anyhow – the horse and cart and the little house and knowing the doll's name. How did we?"

"Lots of times we know things both at once."

"I know, but how did even one of us know it?"

"Oh pooh. Just thought it up, I guess."

"I don't believe it. I don't believe it at all. Anyhow, you wait. There'll be more things. You'll see."

But there weren't. (At least, not before they moved.) Times were too busy. The doll was completely ignored in the last frantic packing days under Mama's tightly organized command.

"You'll feel more at home in Aunt Alice's old house, anyway," Elizabeth told Amelia when she packed her away in the leather box. "You'll like it there."

❧ 4 ❧

Another Dream – And a Pigeon

The first thing Elizabeth thought about on moving day was the little doll. She took it with her on her lap when she left for the big house. Elizabeth left early with Papa and Jane; Mama wanted her weak leg out of the way of the heavy moving and Papa and Jane were to manage the moving in when the furniture van arrived. Privately, knowing how easy it was for Papa to wander off somewhere with his book, Mama gave Jane complete instructions and a written list about which things were to go where and exactly what to do until she, herself, should come with Pat and Joe and William and the last of the furniture.

The day was fair and shining. Dressed for work though they were – Papa in his old khaki pants and faded green shirt, the twins in their jeans, T-shirts, and running shoes – all three felt as though they were on a holiday. With Mama's last-minute instructions about calling the telephone and electricity people still sounding in their ears, Papa began to sing "What Shall We Do With The Drunken Sailor?" Pat's little white dog yipped excitedly in the back seat. Marble sat disdainfully in her corner and noticed no one. Elizabeth drummed her fingers on the lid of Amelia's leather box in time to Papa's singing, and Jane gave up trying to read Mama's list and just looked happily out of the window.

Papa did wander off along the beach with his book. The little dog got lost three times. Jane never managed to decipher Mama's "tbl in lgrm l" or "put chst insfhl" (which Mama told her later, and quite disgustedly, meant the big table was to go on the left side of the living room window and the old chest in the second floor hall). Elizabeth had the distinct impression she was being spied on in the kitchen, which frightened her horribly for a moment (then made her fear, with sinking heart, the new neighborhood was going to have its own Willy Wallet). All the same, the Hubbard family was moved by nighttime.

Mama arrived with Pat, Joe, and William in the back of the last load in the moving van. She was set for an evening of shoving furniture into place, but Papa sent Joe to the Chinese restaurant up on Queen Street to bring home supper. They took it to the beach and ate happily and lazily, watching the sun ease itself into the quiet lake.

After supper the twins went straight to their tower. There was no time and no energy that night to sort out their things. All they did was put their mattresses on the floor for a place to sleep – and one other thing: Elizabeth unpacked the little doll.

"She seems to belong here," she said. She took the doll out of the box and sat her on the wide window seat where she could look out at the lake.

The two girls stood side-by-side, gazing contentedly out through the window. Light was fading from the sky, which was by now a pale orange-pink. Gulls were screeching. Ducks were calling to each other as they settled down for the night. The lake lapped softly against the beach and, down in the garden, Marble was making her way cautiously toward the lilac bush from which were coming young bird sounds.

"Scat," hissed Jane down at the cat. The cat looked disgusted and stalked off toward the coach house. Jane looked at the doll.

"She does look more at home here, you know. I suppose it's because this is an old house and she's an old doll." Thoughtfully Jane licked from her fingers the last of the spareribs she had spirited away from the picnic supper.

"Funny little doll, isn't she? Wonder where she really came from – before the Dolls Mended shop, I mean." Jane picked up the doll.

Before Elizabeth could answer – as if, in fact, the doll were answering for itself – a vision of the little red brick house came to the twins. Not asleep this time, both at once, they saw it, the image of the house, as clearly as though they stood before it on a bright sunny morning. It was a small house with a peak in front trimmed with the carved wood lace painted white. There was a curved window over the low front door, with white curtains; two square windows on either side and a stone step in front. All around the step grew little white and yellow flowers, but the twins hardly noticed those because of the girl standing in the doorway. She was about as tall as they were, with long blond curls and a dress in the style of Amelia's, a brown one with a white collar centered by a gold-etched brooch, which had a large white rose on it surrounded by small colored flowers. The girl had an unpleasant expression on her face, and the twins shared a feeling she was about to say something when the picture began to fade – the way a scene in a movie fades – and disappeared.

They stood there in the half dark looking blankly, first toward the window where the vision had been, then toward each other. The bedroom had darkened to a place of shapes and shadows. The packing boxes, bureau drawers, bedsprings, and coat hangers that had looked funny and out of place a few minutes ago now seemed menacing and mysterious. The bedposts leaning against the far wall had the look of spears or knights' lances. The shadow from the tree outside, bending black and tall as it crossed the built-in window seat, was like the finger of some threatening supernatural giant beckoning them. Aunt Alice's blue and white curtains blew softly in the night breeze.

There seemed to be eyes, unhappy eyes, unfriendly eyes, unkind eyes, watching them, waiting for something.

Suddenly something moved. Something made a soft sound in the night.

Elizabeth was frozen with fright. Jane gasped. She grabbed her sister by the arm.

"What's that?" she whispered. "What's that moaning?" Her words seemed to stick like taffy to the roof of her mouth.

"Poor Lou," came the sound on the edge of a whisper, "poor Lou."

The twins stood there, holding each other tight, the hair on the back of their necks prickling. No words came.

"Poor Lou," again and the sound of the something – or someone – slapping his hands softly together. "P-o-o-rr Lou," right under the window. A shadow moved. Elizabeth screamed.

Suddenly Jane began to laugh, shakily at first and then louder in great gusts. "Oh," she said finally, when she could get her breath, "oh, oh, oh," while Elizabeth sagged against the window and gaped at her.

Jane shoved open the window screen, leaned way out, and looked straight down into just what she expected to see – the round red eye of a large gray pigeon. It stared back at her. She pulled her head in and, wordlessly, Elizabeth thrust hers out to have a look. She began to giggle. Jane began to giggle. They laughed so hard Elizabeth was in danger of falling right out of the window and Jane had to help her back in.

"Oh," said Jane through her bursts of laughter, "oh, there's ghosts and noises for you, oh," and she was off again. They both were. Completely forgetting the doll and the strange experience they had had, they laughed and giggled and laughed some more until they fell exhausted on their mattresses.

5

The Fight

The gleaming sun rays fanned out over the lake and reached their long fingers into all the windows of Aunt Alice's house. The twins were already up, leaning far out of one of their casement windows, investigating the premises of their new friend, Porridge the pigeon. They had given him that name because, said Jane, "he's that color." His nest was just below their window in a round hole in the ivy covering the back of the house. He sat there purriting and poorlouing contentedly. Jane reached into the pocket of her jeans and pulled out a crust of peanut butter sandwich and offered it to him for making friends. He looked at it with a wary eye and made no move to take it. She put it on the window ledge and pulled her head back into the room. He looked at it again, at her, and then, while the twins watched breathlessly, he flapped his wings once, fluttered up to the ledge, picked it up in his bill, and was back in his nest looking quite pleased with himself.

"There," said practical Jane, "there's ghosts and eyes and . . . things that go bump in the night."

Elizabeth laughed remembering the old rhyme Papa used to say to them when they were tiny and afraid of the dark. "All the same," she said, referring to the rest of it, "who knows there mayn't be ghoulies and ghosties. It seemed awfully spooky and anyhow," she faced Jane bringing up the subject she knew her sister had been deliberately avoiding. "What about the doll? and the house? and the girl and everything? Maybe that's not ghoulies and ghosties or mysterious bumps, but it's certainly a funny thing to have happen – a very funny thing!"

"Maybe," Jane shook her head, unconvinced. "But you know it's always been strange being twins. I mean we've always had queer stuff happening that other people don't. You know what I mean." Elizabeth made a face. "You do so," Jane was getting a little cross. "We've always been able to sort of mind read each other. So why is it so odd, if you have a dream, that I see it too. Or the other way around," she added, to even things off.

"Well we never had things like this happen before," insisted Elizabeth, picking up the doll and shaking it a bit. "It has something to do with the doll. I know it has. It has to have. We only started having these funny dreams after we got the doll – and anyway," she turned to Jane, remembering something Jane had never answered, "how did we both know its name is Amelia?"

"It was just a coincidence, a twin thing and . . ."

"And," interrupted Elizabeth, thrusting out her chin, "what about Hester?"

At that moment William's head appeared, coming from the stairwell just at floor level, as though on a platter. Jane let out a little scream.

"Oh," she said, letting out her breath, "it's William."

"Breakfast," said William's head disappearing, and then it was back, "muffins," it added. "Hey! You got a pigeon!"

"Yes," said Elizabeth absently, her mind still fastened to a doll, a small red house, and a girl named Hester.

"Come on," said William's head, and they did. And they didn't return to the doll, the house, and the girl named Hester until the day was done. There wasn't time.

Breakfast in the new house was a comfortable affair, even in the hodgepodge of the day after moving. In the dining room, the bright yellow walls warmly reflected the sunlight pouring through the windows, and shadows from the leaves outside made moving patterns on Marble, sleeping on the window seat. The big oak table Aunt Alice had left for them gave enough room for the whole family and that, along with muffins fresh from the bake shop up on Queen Street, was enough to make everyone rejoice in the day.

"That's a nice little dog you have," Papa said expansively to Patrick. "What's its name?"

"Haven't decided," said Pat, who seemed too absorbed in his breakfast to want to talk much about it.

"How about Claverhouse?" asked Jane brightly, which, for reasons she didn't mention at the time, startled

Elizabeth enough to make her drop her jam. The dog
ate it.

"Not Claverhouse," said Pat definitely.

"Snowball," said Joe. "And I'll take him swimming.
Come on Snowball," and Snowball (if that was to be
his name) looked quite ready to come. But Mama said
quickly, "No swimming, work to do." And that was the end
of the holiday for everyone.

But when evening finally came and the sun lay low over
the lake, the house was beginning to look like a house and
not, as Mama had said in the morning, like the back
storage room at the Salvation Army.

"Nothing wrong with the Salvation Army," Papa had
muttered. "Serves its usefulness." But all the same Mama
had managed to put even Papa to work. Now the sugar
canister was out of the washing machine and on its shelf
between the coffee and the flour, where it belonged. The
hot water bottle was no longer on the mantlepiece in the
living room. The cat's dish had been found in William's
underwear drawer and put beneath the kitchen sink. The
bathroom towels had been taken from the oven and the blue
vase for the pussy willows, which had been at the bottom of
the last packing case, was put in the center of the dining
room table to decorate for supper. As a treat, Mama had
bought a family-sized steak and potato chips to go with it,
and the first whole day in the new house subsided into a
comfortable tiredness of eating and trying once more to
decide what to call Patrick's new dog (which they couldn't

and so left for another day). It was the last comfortable day the twins had for a long time.

When they climbed the stairwell to their tower, twilight had settled on the cherry trees in the garden below. The lake beyond was soft and still. The breeze, much the same breeze that had frightened them the night before, was floating quietly through the windows, disturbing only a very little the blue and white ladies that patterned the curtains.

Elizabeth, standing by the windows looking out at the lake, marshalled the arguments she had been storing all day to convince Jane that something should be done about their dreams. She slid into the conversation gracefully.

"There's a ship in full sail out there. Come see," she invited.

Jane, who always liked to get right down to things, was not deterred by Elizabeth's sideways approach to the conversation.

"I think," she said firmly, resting back on her heels from sorting the paints, books, tennis rackets, and old dolls' clothes, "I think all that dream stuff really is just what Joe said."

"What did Joe say?"

"You know, when we talked about Aunt Alice's sick basket. It's what I said this morning. Twins. We're twins and twins just have the same dreams sometimes."

"No it isn't."

"Twins do."

"I know what twins do and what twins don't do and they don't always have the same dreams. We didn't have the same dreams before we had this doll." She shook the doll impatiently. "Why shouldn't I know what twins do and don't do. You're not the only twin around here."

"Oh," said Jane irritably, "I didn't mean that. I know you're a twin too. I just meant," she said seriously, "I don't think that stuff you were saying this morning about the doll and the dreams is true. . . ."

"Yes it is. It has to be. Look at the dreams, two of them, and knowing names and having feelings – all since we bought the doll. I think the doll wants something, wants us to do something. I really do."

This was too much for Jane. She stood up and marched over to the window where Elizabeth stood holding the doll. "How can a doll want something? Honestly!" She looked closely at the doll's face as she spoke, half expecting it to show some sign that it agreed. She was rather relieved when its bright blue eyes stared impassively back from its cracked face.

"You're always looking for magic, dreaming and imagining things," she said crossly. "Stupid dreams."

"Stupid dreams! You had them too." Elizabeth was outraged. Her face was beginning to show angry red. "You saw the house too and you saw," she paused triumphantly, "you saw Hester. And you know it was Hester. And when I said Hester, and William came up the stairs, you screamed. You did, and I heard you."

Jane started, "I don't even know anyone called Hester," she said lamely.

Someone said, "Ha!" For an instant Jane could have sworn it was the doll, then she looked angrily at Elizabeth.

"Well I don't," she said defensively.

"I don't either," said Elizabeth looking fixedly at her disgruntled sister, "but Amelia does."

"Amelia does?" Jane turned her back to Elizabeth and the doll. "How do you know who Amelia knows? Dolls don't know people anyway. The whole business is just plain silly."

"And how do you know anyhow who I mean when I say Amelia?" and this time Jane knew it was Elizabeth who said, "Ha! Ha!"

"Well, I don't know. I have no idea at all." Jane was as angry as Elizabeth now.

"Oh yes you do!" Elizabeth grabbed Jane's arm. "Yes you do. You just don't want to admit it because . . . because it was my idea. You're just plain hateful." Elizabeth was shaking with rage. "You don't like anything that's interesting or exciting or different at all."

"I don't like what's silly," said Jane coldly, "and I don't see for the least minute why I should be one bit interested in dreams. What's so wonderful about dreams anyway? They aren't real. You can't prove them."

This seemed the ultimate insult for Elizabeth. The one thing Jane could say to make her want to do something wild and murderous.

"Prove it," she screamed. "Prove it. Prove it! PROVE IT! Is that all you can ever say – ever? You can't prove baseball either. Or swimming. Or John A. MacDonald or two and two, but you don't think those are stupid or say prove it to Miss Andrews."

"At least," retorted Jane, spitting out each word with great care, "you can see baseball and John A. MacDonald is in the books and two and two. But your dreams, they're just plain crazy. I wouldn't be one bit surprised if you're crazy. You and your dreams. I don't see at all how I can be twins with someone who's just plain crazy." She walked carefully and deliberately past Elizabeth's nose as though she didn't know Elizabeth or Elizabeth's nose were in the room. She pulled her bathing suit out of the bureau drawer and began to change into it.

"I hate you!" screamed Elizabeth. "I hate being your twin and I hate you. I really truly, absolutely and positively hate YOU!" In her rage she picked up the first thing at hand and hurled it at Jane, who was just starting down the stairs. It was the doll. It landed halfway down where the stairs made a sharp turn. There it stayed, upside down, until Elizabeth crept out of bed much later and retrieved it. She brought it into bed with her then and murmured soothing words to it until finally she fell asleep and dreamed she was with Amelia aboard the sailing ship she had seen out on the lake. The dream was sad.

Jane went with Joe for a quick swim in the dark, but found herself too angry and unhappy to take any pleasure at all from the treat. She slunk into her bed and lay there awake for hours. She couldn't take her mind off the little house or the doll – or Hester. Of course she knew who Hester was, Hester with the brown dress, the puffed sleeves, and the fat brooch. She shivered. She didn't like Hester – and Hester didn't like her either. "That's ridiculous," she whispered into the night. "Who's Hester? How does Hester know me or I know Hester? It's a silly dream. Nothing to do with me. Anyway Hester belongs to the doll, not me. The doll belongs to Hester. Hester belongs to the doll . . . the doll belongs to Hester . . . Hester belongs to the . . . the doll belongs to . . ." and she fell asleep. And dreamed of Hester.

6

Untwins

The fight wasn't over the next day – or the next – or the day after that. The twins couldn't remember a fight that had lasted so long or been so dreadful. They went around for days in silence and hurt and anger. Usually their fights were about something definite, something that happened, but this one was about being twins. It started with the doll, of course – or maybe it was Hester – but it wasn't about that. It was about being twins, being different but locked together by shared thoughts, feelings – and now dreams. They wanted to break that lock. They wanted to so badly they could barely speak.

"Mama, are Liza and Jane untwins?" William asked and the family decided maybe that's what they were, untwins.

Feeling sorry and hoping to make things more comfortable in the family, Mama suggested that one of them move to the attic room. Neither twin, knowing how much the other loved the tower room, would do this.

So Jane went off every morning down the beach to the high diving pool. Two days in a row she brought home a girl named Polly, who lived a couple of streets away, and ignored Elizabeth strenuously.

Elizabeth did more or less the same thing. She didn't dive. She puttered around, found the local library, and got to know Miss Porcastle, the librarian. She tried dressmaking for the doll, but after three unsuccessful attempts she left it with its half-made clothes in the window seat. Although she couldn't actually put it right out of her head, she shoved it into the background and concentrated on historical novels under the cherry tree.

Papa tried to show his sympathy by taking them for a walk, but neither wanted his sympathy.

It was the doll that ended the fight – which was only fair since it was the doll that had begun it.

Elizabeth went upstairs at noon, a day or so after the nighttime walk, to get away from Mama's cross scolding. Someone had been at Mama's sewing, and since Elizabeth had lately shown some interest in sewing, Mama had questioned her closely about it. Indignantly Elizabeth had denied all knowledge of the mess. Hurt, she had gone upstairs to her own room. As she often did these days, she went to the window seat to tell Amelia all about it. Amelia wasn't there. She looked in the space inside the window seat. The doll wasn't there either, nor in the closet, nor on the chair, nor any other place in the room.

Back to the window seat she went in panic, to have another look. From the window she could see Jane coming up the garden walk. Forgetting they were untwins, not sharing things, not speaking at all, she raced down the stairs and slammed through the kitchen door.

"Oh, Jane," she cried, nearly running her sister down, "it's gone."

Without stopping to ask what, Jane looked up toward the window.

"No it isn't," she said. "There it is."

Elizabeth whirled round on her heel, looked up where Jane was pointing. There was Amelia, face down into the pigeon hole, hanging by one foot from the window ledge above.

The twins stared at each other, their fight forgotten.

"How did you know?" Elizabeth asked.

"I don't know. I just knew what you were looking for and I knew where it was clear as day."

"The doll . . ." Elizabeth was about to say triumphantly, *the doll told you*, but she cut off the words before she could say them. Elizabeth had learned something.

"I wonder how it got there," she said.

"Maybe Porridge took it. Maybe he thought it was to eat – you know, like the peanut butter sandwich."

From high up in his pigeon hole Porridge regarded them out of his unblinking eyes.

"I'll bet that's what he did," said Elizabeth, somehow relieved.

From behind them William said, "Maybe Porridge wants your doll for his babies to play with."

Jane and Elizabeth burst out laughing.

"Oh, William," Jane said, "he birds don't have babies," but when Jane went upstairs and leaned out of the window to rescue Amelia, she looked down into the nest and William was right. Porridge had babies.

"Maybe he – or I guess it's she – did want it for her babies," she said breathlessly when she was back beside the cherry tree, the doll clutched safely in her hands.

The twins looked at each other warily. Jane said quickly, "I'llbefriendsifyouwill," which was a make-up-after-a-fight formula they had been using, almost since they had started talking real words.

And Elizabeth quickly gave the expected answer, "Guessitwasn'tallyourfault," and solemnly they shook hands. To cover their embarrassment they sat down under the tree to talk about Porridge and her babies.

7

To Find a House

All that afternoon, Jane and Elizabeth sat under the cherry tree in the back garden. William watched them curiously for a brief while and then went off to find his cars. Joe came by and threw a handful of sand at them on his way from the beach. Patrick passed on his way from cleaning the coach house, and the puppy, following Pat, decided he liked the shade of the cherry tree and squeezed in between the twins.

Jane had learned something from the fight, too. She had made up her mind – suddenly, on her way upstairs to rescue Amelia – to go along with Elizabeth's ideas. Being untwins was too painful. She was going to try, really try, to see things Elizabeth's way. And if Elizabeth wanted to start a crazy hunt for the things in the dreams, she was going to do it and she wasn't going to say a word about how stupid it was. If it killed her, she promised herself, she would do it – and she felt much better for deciding.

"OK," she said, "maybe you're right about the doll. Maybe there IS something about it. Maybe we SHOULD do something."

Elizabeth was overjoyed. "Oh Jane, there is, there really is. Listen," she sat up on her heels and wound the ends of her hair around her fingers with excitement. "What I think is that long ago when Amelia was new she was Hester's doll and lived in that house."

Jane shivered.

"I know what you mean," Elizabeth put her hand on Jane's arm. "There's something about Hester, isn't there? Something not nice. But she's part of it and we have to think about her. It was her house."

"I'd rather think about the doll."

"She wants us to find it."

"What?"

"The house."

"Who does?"

"The doll, stupid."

"Oh, Elizabeth," Jane began and stopped herself, remembering her pledge. "Well," she said hastily, "if it's true and the doll wants us to find the dream house, how do we do it? If she's as old as she looks, she must be hundreds of years old. We can't go back hundreds of years just like that and find it – and where was it anyway? Toronto isn't hundreds of years old. Remember in history last year we took Toronto. It's a lot newer than lots of places. What if the house was in England or France or somewhere?"

"Oh, no. It couldn't have been. It must have been here." Elizabeth was emphatic.

"Why?"

"Because the doll's here. We found it here. It has its dreams here."

Jane swallowed carefully the part about the doll having dreams and said, "It could have come from somewhere else."

"But it found us here. It wasn't just an accident, us going into that shop. It found us here because here is where it wants us to look for its house."

"All right," said Jane. There didn't seem to be much point in arguing.

"What do we do," she asked, rolling over on top of the happy puppy snuggled in between them, "hire a time machine? Or will the doll take care of it? If we hire a time machine, Claverhouse," she murmured into the dog's white fur, "we'll take you, too, OK?"

Elizabeth looked suspiciously at her sister, "You don't need to make fun," she said.

"Wasn't really," Jane jumped up and so did the dog, looking hopefully for someone to romp with. "I just don't entirely see how we're going to manage it, that's all – get down Claverhouse."

There was a look of triumph in Elizabeth's eyes. "Why do you call that dog Claverhouse?" she asked.

"I don't know, just came to me that it would be a good name."

"I think Hester had a dog named Claverhouse."

This was almost too much for Jane. She was sure Elizabeth had made that up, but having made up her mind to do a thing, Jane was not one to give up easily. Hastily she changed the subject; "Really, Eliza, we can't find a house and a girl from long ago times. It isn't possible."

"We'll have to go house hunting," answered her sister imperturbably. "We'll go into town and look at all the houses. There can't be many exactly like Hester's."

Mama was pleased the next morning when the twins asked if they could go uptown. "I'm glad to have you out of the way," she said, "not messing in my kitchen or my sewing things." (*That's the second time*, thought Elizabeth and promised herself to speak to William.) She gave them an errand to do in the wool shop on Temperance Street and threatened them with horrifying consequences if they were not home on time.

They went upstairs, put on their matching red and white striped dresses ("People are always more helpful when we dress alike," said Elizabeth. Jane snorted but obeyed.), and off they went to the streetcar to look for Hester's house.

At first they saw nothing that resembled the house in their dream. Then they saw a row with white peaks in the front but too tall, and then nothing. On they went for a mile or so, peering from this side of the streetcar and then that, expecting at any moment to see their house (at least Elizabeth did) – and then Elizabeth saw it. She was sure she did. It was thin and little, old, with dirty paint, but still, unmistakably, a little red brick house with a white wood lace peak at its front. Jane leading, they hurried off the streetcar. Jane didn't know what to think seeing the house really standing there. She started across the street.

"Wait," Elizabeth hadn't moved. "It's not right," she said sadly.

"Don't be silly."

"No, it isn't," Elizabeth shook her head. It was a deep disappointment to her but she knew she was right.

"You mean because it's so shabby?"

"No, I know it would have to be old-looking now. No, it isn't that – something else and it hasn't got the butter-and-eggs. I guess they'd die after a while, too." This house not only had no little white and yellow flowers by its doorstep, it had nothing but soot and dirt clinging to every part of it. "No." said Elizabeth again, "I know what it is. It's the lace. The lace is wrong." She pointed toward the house's peaked trim. "Our house has two circles or some-thing. This one has a tulip. See?"

Jane did. Where the white wood trim came together to form its point it curled around at the bottom in the shape of a tulip.

"Ours has roses, I think," she said.

"Yes, roses," agreed Elizabeth thoughtfully, "roses, I'm sure. Oh, dear! Well we'll have to get on the next streetcar and look some more. Have we got any more money?"

"Enough for that, I guess," and they got on the next streetcar and resumed their watch. Jane on one side of the car, Elizabeth on the other.

This time it was Jane who saw the house, but before rushing off the streetcar they both looked at its white peak. Alas, the lace trim had a design in fern shape, no flower petals of any kind. Then Elizabeth saw another little house, and another. Jane saw a whole row – all shabby, all old, but none with the double rose design they remembered from the dream. By the time the streetcar had run all across town, they had seen twenty-seven single houses with white wood lace peaks and nine whole rows of them.

"It's sort of like the tinderbox story," said Elizabeth disconsolately, "with the X on one door and then X's on all the other doors in town. We'll never find it."

"Why didn't we ever see any houses like this before?" Jane leaned her tired head back on the car seat, wishing she were home going swimming.

"I don't know. Maybe it's because we were never looking for one. I never noticed anyone else's broken leg before I broke mine, but the first day I went out with a cast I saw five."

"Funny," said Jane but she didn't sound as though she meant it. "I guess we'll go home now."

"I guess so," said Elizabeth. "We can try again tomorrow and maybe we should bring the doll."

"What for?"

"To help remember, stupid."

Jane groaned inwardly but closed her eyes and said no more. It wasn't until they were within one stop of their own street that they remembered Mama's errand. They had to go all the way back to town for it and were forty minutes late getting home.

Their mother was cross, not only because of their being late, but because she had discovered her dressing table in a complete hash of jewelry, lipstick, and cologne.

"Look," she said, "I don't know what's got into you girls. You've never been like this before, never. If you want my needles, cloth, lipstick, hairpins – anything – just ask. I was patient those days you were so unhappy but I've spoken to you several times now – this is just too much."

"But we didn't. We . . ."

"No buts. Who else in the family would bother with jewelry and make-up like that?" and she sent them to their room without dinner.

Hot, tired, and put out by this injustice, the twins posted themselves at the windows hoping to see someone who would get them something to eat. While they waited they went over their afternoon and decided it hadn't been a total waste of time. They had learned one thing: Toronto was full of their kind of house. They were looking in the right place.

"Tomorrow we'll take Amelia." Elizabeth reached inside the window seat to get the doll out. "Boy," she said, "what a mess. Why did you dump all these things in here?" She pulled the doll out from under a jumble of paints and tennis shoes.

"I didn't." Jane was indignant. And then she saw Joe through the back window.

"Joe," she hissed.

"What?" He shouted up.

"Shh!"

"What is it?" – a loud whisper.

"Come here a minute, but please be quiet."

"OK," he shouted again and soon his head appeared above the floor from the stairwell. "What do you want?"

"We can't have supper. If I give you some money, will you get us a hot dog or something?"

"Why can't you?"

"Oh never mind. Will you get the things?"

"If you tell me first."

"Oh, OK. The dog or someone knocked over all Mama's stuff on her dressing table and she thinks it's us – and it isn't – but she won't let us have any supper. So here's a quarter. You could get a hot dog or something and we could split it."

"You twins . . ."

"You're a good kid, Joe," Elizabeth said quickly. "And we'll time your swimming if you go."

Joe went. Jane watched out the window and a few minutes later Claverhouse – or Snowball – came bouncing along beside Joe as he whistled his way up the street.

"Papa's right," Jane said, "the dog is getting bigger and bigger. I wonder how big he'll be when he's finished?"

"Don't know." Elizabeth was under the bed searching for a piece of chocolate bar she thought she might have left there.

"Look at that boat. Oh Elizabeth, come look. It's terrific – just like the old-fashioned sailing ships."

"Mhm," Elizabeth came up regretfully from under her bed where she had found no chocolate. "I guess that's the same one I saw the other night. It's gorgeous. I'm hungry."

It wasn't more than five minutes before Joe's whistling came back down the street.

"I wonder what he's got?" said Elizabeth hopefully. There's much more than a hot dog or a chocolate bar in that big bag.

"I guess," said Jane, "he had to shop for Mama."

But when Joe appeared a few moments later, he still had the same big bag with him.

"Pat had some dough," he explained with a grin, "and I had an extra dime, so we got some more," and he pulled out of the bag, like a magician pulling rabbits from a high hat, potato chips, four hot dogs, two coconut cakes wrapped in cellophane and two bottles of orange soda pop.

"Yippee," cried Jane. "Oh Joe you're great!"

"I'll give you a kiss," offered Elizabeth, but Joe said no thanks and retreated hastily down the stairwell.

Stuffing themselves with hot dogs and potato chips the twins returned to the doll. Jane said maybe they ought to leave it alone for a few days, but Elizabeth was determined to go back downtown the next day with Amelia and look again for the house.

"OK, then," said Jane, "we'll make a list."

"Make a list?"

"The way detectives do in detective books – it's sort of a detectivy thing anyway, isn't it? I mean, we have some clues and we have to find a missing thing."

Elizabeth put down the coconut cakes, still unwrapped, and looked at her sister suspiciously, "You mean organize?" she accused. "Oh no, no lists. We'll just go back downtown with the doll and just let her show us the way."

"You mean like one of those people looking for well water with a stick?" Jane was incredulous.

"I suppose, sort of."

Jane remembered again why it was she was looking for the house in the first place and said nothing. She picked up the coconut cakes and began to take off the cellophane.

It was at this moment Mama called from downstairs.

"I've been thinking it over," she said when they stood before her in the kitchen. "I think perhaps I was a little harsh with you. I suppose it could have been the puppy in my dressing table. In any case I feel I should take your word for it. You may have your supper."

For a moment neither girl said anything. Then Jane said with a gulp, "Thank you," and together they meekly followed their mother into the dining room.

"It's hot dogs," said Joe gleefully passing them the platter, "and potato chips."

Patrick said nothing but the twins could see by his eyes that he thought it was just as funny as Joe did.

"What's wrong?" asked Mama, looking from one to the other of them.

"Nothing," said Joe, looking hard at William and biting into his hot dog. No one else said anything.

"Aren't you going to eat?" asked Papa in a tone that said clearly, *no sulks*, and the twins valiantly ate one hot dog, a small dish of coleslaw, and three potato chips each. At least that's what it looked like. Jane fed all of hers to the dog, and Elizabeth got rid of most of hers the same way until Papa caught the dog with the end of it, accused him of having stolen it, and insisted on getting Elizabeth another one.

"That dog," he said, giving the animal a hard look, "seems bigger and bigger to me. Patrick," he asked, "how old is the dog?"

"Well," said Pat, and you could see he was uncomfortable. For the first time since the dog had come into the family, Papa was giving it his full attention (what Joe called the treatment).

"I don't know a great deal about dogs," Papa continued, not waiting for Pat's reply, "but I have always believed that full-grown dogs do not run about as much as this one – and another thing," he looked suspiciously from Patrick to the dog and back again, "the only dog I've ever encountered with hair like that, growing right down into its eyes, was an English sheep dog."

"Sheep dog," gasped Mama. Over on the window seat Marble sat up. "But sheep dogs grow as big as horses!"

"Yes," said Papa ominously, "they do. Well Patrick?" Everyone looked at Pat.

"Yes," said Patrick, "they do."

"Is this dog going to be a sheep dog when it's fully grown?" Papa demanded.

"Well," Pat said, "I guess . . . I guess . . . maybe it will be. . . ."

"What do you mean, you guess? Is it a sheep dog now?"

"Well, yes."

"I thought as much. Your mother is right. Do you know how big sheep dogs are when they're full-grown?"

"Yes."

"Yes, I suppose that's a foolish question since you spend more of your time with dogs than you do with people. I'm sure you must be aware of the relative sizes of dogs. A horse. A horse." Papa paused. Nobody spoke. He went on, "The last sheep dog I had any acquaintance with belonged to a farmer who had the next farm to my grandfather. He had sheep too," added Papa meditatively. "That sheep dog used to pull the pigs around in a cart when my sister Dora put them there and when he got into the rose garden, my grandfather . . . oh, he was a VERY large dog. . . ." Papa's voice trailed off for a moment into memory.

"We do have the coach house in the back," Patrick offered weakly when he thought it was safe to speak.

The dog, who may or may not have realized he was being discussed in such a manner that his whole future might depend on the conversation, wandered over to the window seat, put out his tongue, and licked Marble a lick that covered her entire face.

Marble – to whom such a thing had never before happened – opened her eyes in great surprise, arched her back, flattened it again, and began to wash the dog's ears.

"Well," said Papa, after a long pause, "I guess that settles it. If those two creatures can get along in this house without fighting – and they, heaven knows, are the only ones who can," he looked pointedly at the twins, "then the dog stays. You may call him Horse." Papa got up and left the dining room.

8

More House Hunting – And Two Roses

For the next few days Jane and Elizabeth went on fifteen different streetcar rides and walked, it seemed, miles and miles of city streets, looking for an old red brick house with a double rose pattern in its trim. They saw hundreds of red brick houses with the now familiar peak of carved wood – some crumbled and half fallen in, some with shops or laundries built into their fronts, some in good repair with their white wood painted and bright, some that looked as though they might once have been red brick but now painted yellow or gray and made fresh and handsome with flowers in their window boxes. Not one of all those hundreds was the house they were looking for. Amelia's house. Hester's house.

The days were getting hot with cloudless skies and pavements like hot griddle pans. Jane was tired of walking, tired of looking for a house she was sure they wouldn't find. She never said so, but oh, how she wanted to be spending those days on the sand and in the water. Elizabeth's determination never lagged. She held the doll tightly in her hand all the time they searched and, unlike Jane, who systematically examined the houses they passed for size, shape, and roses in their peaks, Elizabeth depended entirely on the feelings she had toward them – she counted on Amelia to let her know. But after four days of steady hunting, even she was beginning to get discouraged when her only real feeling of finding something turned out to be the back of an old theater, in no way at all resembling the little brick house.

Around noon on the fifth day out, very hot, very tired, with fifteen cents in their combined pockets, the twins were ready to go home. They were walking along College Street past the Central Library, heads down, not saying anything, when suddenly they bumped into their father hurrying in the opposite direction.

Papa was on his way to have lunch and he took them with him. Settled comfortably around the table in the little restaurant, hamburgers and milkshakes in front of them, the twins told Papa something of the hunt they were on. Neither was sure how much to tell or how to tell it, but they both thought maybe Papa could help.

"You see," Elizabeth explained, "we found this old doll." She showed Papa the doll and he examined it carefully.

"That is old," he said, "and I should think fairly valuable. Where on earth did you find it?"

Jane told about the Antiques, Dolls Mended shop. Papa looked surprised.

"Well," he said, "I could be wrong. If the woman in the antique shop sold it to you for two dollars and fifty-five cents it can't be too valuable. She must know her business. Maybe it's a later copy of an old doll that's been badly treated. Still, I would have sworn . . ." He picked up the doll again. "Hm, in any case," he handed it back to Elizabeth with a smile, "that's not really your problem, is it?"

Elizabeth thought hard for a minute, sucking on her milkshake.

"You see," she said carefully, "we got interested in the doll and we wanted to know about Toronto and houses and things at the time the doll was new. You know, we sort of wanted to dress it up new ("As if it were new, or as it was when it was new," corrected Papa.) as it was when it was new," Elizabeth obliged, "and sort of find out some-thing about the times – the olden times, I mean."

"We found it interesting," Jane added self-consciously.

"So how do we do that?" Elizabeth looked guilelessly at her father.

"Well now," Papa leaned back in his chair and took out his pipe, "you want to know something about old Toronto. I could sit here for hours and tell you things but maybe they wouldn't be the things you'd like to hear, and I really haven't the time, so perhaps you'd better start on a research project. Go to the library, go to the museum, ask for the information available about your subject. Then look around the city in the spots the books suggest and you'll find many of the old houses still standing." The twins didn't have the courage to tell him they had already seen all too many.

"If you run into a snag," Papa continued, "come back to me and I'll help you with it. In the meanwhile, look things up, make notes, and gather all your information before you start looking again."

"But that's organizing," said Elizabeth, outraged.

Papa laughed. "Organizing can be a good thing, Liza," he said. "If you want to find out things you have to organize your material – sort out what you know before you can make any sense of it."

Jane tried not to look smug.

"Come on. I have to go up to the museum myself. I'll take you along and you can ask about clothes and houses there," Papa offered.

The museum was almost as frustrating as their four-and-a-half day tramp had been. There were many dresses, many brooches like the one Hester wore in the dream, fashionable, said the labels, about 120 years ago. It was harder to tell about the doll's clothes because hers were so badly worn, but it seemed that her dress, like Hester's, was from the period of the 1840s.

"That's something to know, anyhow," Jane said encouragingly as they got off the subway from the museum and stood waiting for the Queen streetcar to take them home.

Elizabeth didn't hear Jane. Jane had disappeared. The city had disappeared. She was standing in a field of tall grass, with cows grazing around her. There were children there, too, in dresses and pants like the clothes they had just seen in the museum. The summer wind was blowing high and everyone was running, laughing. She stooped to put down her doll to run with them. She opened her mouth to say, "Wait, I'm coming," when she was pulled abruptly away. The children were gone. The field was gone. The only thing that looked the same was the heavy iron fence. Jane was pulling her arm. The streetcar was coming.

"Come on," she said, "What's the matter with you?"

"Nothing." Elizabeth wanted to think a little about what she'd seen before she told.

When they got home and Jane suggested once more, as a result of what Papa had said about research, that they make a list of the things they knew, Elizabeth didn't argue. They sat down on the beach with a pencil and paper after they had had a swim and Jane wrote:

Things we know about Amelia:
1. She is old, about 120-150 years old.

"We don't know that exactly," interjected Elizabeth. "No," answered Jane impatiently, "but we can start with that."

2. She lived in a red brick house with a white peak and two roses in it.
3. Hester lived there too.

"We don't know that for sure," said Elizabeth.
"Sure we do, what makes you say that?"

"I don't know, I just feel that way."

Jane kept her thoughts about that to herself.

4. Amelia came in a leather box, also old.

"Where is the box?" she asked, not looking up from her writing.

"Upstairs. I'll get it."

While Elizabeth was gone, Jane put down her pencil and looked longingly toward the lake. She wondered just how long she was going to be able to keep up the nonsense. Instead of feeling closer to Elizabeth she was finding her sister harder and harder to understand. *Oh, well*, she thought. *It is an old doll and maybe we will find out some interesting things.* Elizabeth came bounding out of the kitchen door, racing through the garden.

"Guess what?" she shouted as she ran. "Guess what? It's roses. The box has two roses, look!" She threw herself down on the sand beside Jane and thrust the box under her sister's eyes. There on the long catch of the leather box were two roses, side-by-side. Jane had been right. The flower petal designs on the peak of the brick house were roses, roses just like the ones on Amelia's box.

9

Jane Is Frightened

The roses were a great shock to Jane. She was silent all evening. She let Elizabeth do all the talking. Excited talking. Insane talking. Talking about magic, about visiting back in time, about signs leading the way to fantastic discoveries and about mental telepathy. Jane hated it. It frightened her. What if Elizabeth was right? She had restless dreams all night, and first thing in the morning she poked her leg out of bed and gave her sister a shove with her toe.

Elizabeth humped over in her own bed. "Whmph marr?" she asked into her pillow.

"Wake up."

"Why?" Elizabeth rolled over, sat up, reached down, and touched her toes. She had once heard it made girls graceful so she had been doing it every morning for three years. With toes touched twice she slumped back in her bed.

"Why should I wake up?"

"I just wanted company," Jane grinned as Elizabeth hurled her pillow across the space between the beds and hit her in the face. (They had had their bunk beds made into single beds when they moved into the tower room.)

"Liza," Jane added seriously, "I have a feeling something not nice is going to happen. You know, sort of like having a test in school or going to the dentist or something. Do you feel that way, too?"

"No, but I know what your horrible feeling is all about. Willy Wallet is coming today."

Jane groaned, "Oh, I'd forgotten all about that. Why did you have to remind me?" She got out of bed and walked over to the window.

"You asked," answered Elizabeth cheerfully. "Are we going to the library this morning to look at some more houses?"

Jane didn't want to. She wasn't sure she wanted to find out anything more but, being Jane, she couldn't leave it unfinished either.

"Yes," she said, with a carefully repressed sigh, "we'll go."

Downstairs in the garden, Papa was having his after-breakfast coffee.

"How's it going?" he asked. "How's the history project?"

"Not too well," Jane answered, then said quickly, "but we're really finding out lots of things."

"Does the library have books of families?" Elizabeth interrupted.

"Books of families?" Papa was puzzled.

"You know, books with names of people in old Toronto families?"

"You may have to go into the Canadian or the Ontario archives for that – those are the official records – but try the library certainly. Why do you want those? Are you going to write a story or something?" Papa smiled indulgently.

"Maybe," Elizabeth said and was looking around for a way out of the discussion when Horse came bounding around the corner of the house and jumped into Papa's lap, spilling the last of the coffee into the grass.

Papa leapt out of his chair, glaring at the dog. "No peace in this house at all," he shouted, "no peace in this family, ever." He stomped off toward the kitchen.

"Come on, Horse," said Jane, "I'll give you a ride," and she coaxed him into William's wagon and began to pull him round and round the garden while he barked and waggled with joy, until Mama came out of the kitchen to see what the noise was all about and Joe came around the corner followed by Willy Wallet.

"Where did you get that goat?" Willy asked, and right away Jane remembered all the things about Willy she particularly didn't like.

"Oh shut up," she said and went into the kitchen. Elizabeth went too.

They decided, sitting in the kitchen eating bacon and eggs, that Willy Wallet's being there was all the more reason for going to the library. Jane asked Elizabeth if she had really wanted to know about books of families or was she just helping the conversation out. Elizabeth said she really wanted to know.

"You know," she said, "if we find a family with the name Hester somewhere in it, it would be a great clue, wouldn't it? I mean there can't be too many Hesters can there?"

"You mean like red brick houses with white wood lace trim?" asked Jane.

Elizabeth agreed her sister had made a point, but they thought they might as well look anyway and off they went to the local library.

Miss Porcastle said hello to Elizabeth and remarked about how nice it was to see two such charming girls ("twins, aren't you dears?") so interested in history. She sat them down at a table in the corner and began to bring them books.

"How many do you want, dear?" she asked.

"As many as you've got," answered Jane firmly.

Miss Porcastle looked doubtful but back she went and brought more and more books until the twins were almost hidden behind them. All morning they looked through the mountain of books, page by page, book by book. They found pictures of people, streets, shops, but never a sign of Hester's house. They looked for names and found lots of those too – including, to Elizabeth's chagrin, plenty of Hesters. Finally they couldn't look at another picture or read another page, and they got up and went home with nothing accomplished.

At least Jane felt there had been nothing accomplished. Elizabeth felt strongly that some of the pictures she had seen in the books were places the doll might have remembered. She thought of telling Jane about her experience the day before at the streetcar stop but decided to wait. Now she had seen so many pictures, she wanted to check the doll's clothes again, to look at it more carefully to be sure it belonged to the time they thought it did.

As soon as they got home, Elizabeth went right upstairs to get the doll, but, when she reached into the window seat to find it, the doll wasn't there.

"That's funny," said Jane.

"No, it's not," cried Elizabeth, "no it's not. Jane, there's something wrong. I know there's something wrong!"

"What do you mean, wrong?" asked Jane from outside the window. She was looking in the pigeon hole.

"I mean someone or something's trying to take our doll away."

"Don't be silly," came the answer, "Say – there are two pigeon holes down here, one just a little ways over from Porridge's."

"Is the doll in it?"

"No."

"Then why did you tell me that?" Elizabeth was aggrieved. "What's that got to do with our doll? I tell you, Jane Hubbard, someone's trying to take our doll."

"Who'd want it, or why?" Jane's head was back inside the room.

"I don't know, maybe it's valuable. Remember what Papa said?"

"Oh, valuable," Jane said scornfully. "Remember Papa said that it couldn't be, it must be a cheap copy or something?"

"Well, I don't care, all I know is that it's missing and I want it."

Jane had an inspiration. "We'll ask William. William always sees everything."

"All right," Elizabeth agreed, somewhat mollified.

William was out on the beach just beyond the garden where he had made a most marvelous and elaborate system of roads. There were highways and streets, underground tunnels and sweeping overpasses, popsicle sticks for street lights, and all along were his cars and trucks. Over at one side, like a benevolent fairy watching over the entire scene, was the wooden doll.

"William!" said Elizabeth in outrage and relief, "where did you get our doll?"

William looked up in surprise. "I found it by the lilac bush," he said, "so I thought it would be all right if I played with it. It's the Friendly Car Spirit of the North."

"That's east," said Jane automatically, "and anyway it wasn't . . ."

"It wasn't by the lilac bush, and you know it," said Elizabeth indignantly, grabbing it. "It was up in our room on the window seat."

"No it wasn't," William insisted. "It was under the lilac bush – way under it. Please, Liza," his tone changed to one

74

of pleading, "can I have it to be the Friendly Car Spirit of the North?"

Elizabeth looked at Jane who shrugged. In a way, Elizabeth was glad to let William have it. She felt no one on earth would be a better guardian so she said, "OK, but guard it with your life. I'm going to have lunch."

A little while later, when the two of them were finishing lemonade and peanut butter sandwiches under the cherry tree, Elizabeth made a pronouncement. "I'm going to think," she declared.

Jane groaned. She knew what that meant. Elizabeth's think spells nearly drove her wild. When Jane had a problem, she wanted to do things – write lists, clean the room, make muffins, or play baseball. When Elizabeth had a problem, she had a think spell. "I just want to think," she would say, and then she would lie, usually on her back with her head hanging over the side of her bed until her face was beet red, and think until she pronounced herself thought out. Then she would get up. It irritated Jane, who was sure it never solved anything, and besides, didn't allow her to talk all the time it was going on.

"Please don't think," she pleaded. "We've found the doll now and it wasn't something ghostly or anything."

"Ghoulies and ghosties and things that go bump in the night," chanted William on his way past.

"Go away William," said Jane.

"It was only William playing roads with it," Jane continued. "We can go back to the library," she coaxed, "take the doll along if you like and . . ."

"Can't go anywhere," announced Mama, coming out of the door in her good white suit and her blue straw hat. "I'm going to see Aunt Alice, and you're going to stay here and mind William. And," she added, pulling on her gloves, "no getting into fights with the boys."

"Boys," said the twins in one voice, "where are they?"

"Swimming, but they'll probably be home soon. Now behave," and Mama disappeared around the corner.

"Probably," said Jane disgustedly, "probably will."

"I'll think," said Elizabeth, starting to get up.

"No wait," said Jane, "why don't we go on making our list. Remember we had only got started when . . ."

"When we found the roses," Elizabeth sat down again. "Well, we don't really know any more things, do we?"

"Still, detectives don't either when they start solving a mystery."

"Maybe we should get Sherlock Holmes hats and magnifying glasses," Elizabeth giggled. She inched herself along on her stomach until her top half was completely shaded by the cherry tree and her bottom half was under the lilac bush. "I could think right here," she murmured.

Jane got up. "If you're going to go on and on and on about that," she said crossly, "I'm going swimming."

"Can't. Have to mind William."

The afternoon looked as though it might deteriorate into another fight. The sun was hot. No breeze moved the leaves in the cherry tree or the lilac bush. In the distance, people were shouting and splashing in the lake, but right there in the garden no creature moved. Even Horse had settled himself way under the lilac bush opposite Elizabeth, burrowing deeper and deeper until he had found what was probably the only cool spot in Ontario.

"All right," Jane started to say, "I'll let you think," when Joe and Willy burst into the yard with glad shouts and began to snap dirty wet towels at them.

"Oh, go away," said Elizabeth crossly, which was like an invitation to a feast for those two boys.

"Ho! Ho!" sang Willy, and Joe, of course, followed suit, flinging towels even more wildly.

"Come on, let's play tag. Come on Joe, let's play tag with the girls. You're it," he punched Jane on the arm.

"I am not," she said haughtily, "going to play games with little children. Go ask William to play," whereupon Willy began to snap his towel at her so that it would really hurt, and she ran into the house shouting all the way, "Stop it you miserable little boy."

Up the stairs she ran and Willy chased her. Fleeing the snapping towel, she ran toward the upstairs front porch. Willy headed her off. Turning along the hall, she ran down the steps to the unused room that was once the attic, raced inside, and slammed the door shut after her. Close behind, Willy turned the old key in the lock. Jane heard it clatter to the floor as he marched away, saying as he went, "Now spend the afternoon in the hot box and say all the things you like spitey-tongue, ha, ha!" She was well and truly locked in the old attic.

Out of breath and confused, she thought she was some-where else, in a room with flower-striped wallpaper and loosely woven white curtains at the window. When her breath returned, she could see it was really the attic, dusty, dingy, gray, with a fat beam going up the center of it and one shutter hanging loose from the curtainless window. *Wishful thinking, I guess*, she decided.

At first she waited, listening to the sounds of Willy and Joe chasing Elizabeth toward the water, trying to throw her in. After a few moments there was a scream, a splash that told her they had been successful, a great horselaugh, and then silence. Jane knew she was abandoned.

She looked about her curiously, wondering what about the room had given her the impression it had flowers on its wall. "It's black and almost burned-looking," she said to herself. And it did look as though there might once have been a fire. The beams near the window looked quite charred, although they were so black with age no one could really tell. The whole attic was black and bleak. It was the most depressing place Jane had ever been in. She began to feel as though there were eyes watching her – *like the night we found Porridge*, she thought and smiled. But the smile soon faded and the eyes were still there. There was some-thing in the attic, something in the dark attic that didn't like her. She was sure of it. She had to get away. She ran to the window – the one glow of light.

"It can't have been opened in years and years," she gasped, shoving against it with all her weight. Fear made her strong, and with one creak the window flew up. Jane, flung forward by her own strength, just missed falling out. She clutched the window to save herself and breathed the freshness of the outside air.

Down below William was trying to ride a very reluctant Horse.

"William," called Jane weakly.

He looked up.

"Please," she whispered, "come open the attic door. Willy Wallet's locked me in."

"All right." William disappeared and in a minute or two was outside the attic fiddling with the key.

Gratefully Jane slumped through the door and down the stairs. William stood looking curiously inside for a couple of minutes and then he too came away.

She found Elizabeth in the tower room – thinking. When Jane hadn't reappeared from Willy's chase, Elizabeth assumed she had gone swimming. With the idea still firmly fixed in her mind that she needed a think to solve their problem, she had taken the doll and gone upstairs. But it hadn't worked. She had tried standing on her head, sitting with her hands touching the doll lightly as though it were a ouija board, concentrating with all her might on the little red house, and finally, lying on her bed with her head hung backward over the edge. It had all been no use.

"The only odd thing that happened," she told Jane, "was that I thought for a moment that I saw you in an old-fashioned bedroom with roses on the wallpaper, but it went away so soon I'm not sure about it now."

It was almost too much for Jane. She didn't say anything. She couldn't tell that she had seen it too. Not right then. She had to think about if for a while first. She put on her bathing suit and went swimming, trying to throw off the edges of fear that still clung to her.

"It wasn't really the attic," she told herself unhappily as she swam with strong, even strokes out from the beach, "it's the doll and all those funny things." Jane could no longer convince herself that those funny things were Elizabeth's imaginings or that she was hunting Hester's house to please her sister. There was something strange going on. She knew it now. She didn't like it, but she knew too that she would have to do everything she possibly could to find out what it was. How else would anything ever again make sense? When she was too exhausted to swim any more, she came in, still not happy.

Late that night Horse set up such a lot of barking out near the coach house it woke Jane from a muddled dream. She sat up, saw Marble sitting straight up tall in a patch of moonlight on the window seat beside the doll, and lay down again, glad Horse was in the coach house and Marble standing guard at the window.

❧ 10 ❧

Jane Makes Up Her Mind

Jane said nothing to anyone about the barking in the night or Marble's strange behavior, but she was badly frightened. It had come to her in the dark and muddle of her dreams that they, she and Elizabeth, had brought ghosts to Aunt Alice's house. In the morning she felt foolish. *There aren't ghosts*, she told herself crossly. *There aren't. Maybe there are dreams and maybe they mean something even, but it doesn't mean there are ghosts.* But she didn't entirely believe the things she told herself. Ever since the roses had shown up on the old leather box, she had been shaken and unsure. Ever since yesterday afternoon in the attic, she hadn't been able to throw off the uneasiness that clung to her like a smothering velvet cloth. There was something wrong. Something was going to happen. Against all sense and reason she knew something was going to happen.

There was a heaviness in the air, which didn't help Jane's mood at all. Already, at seven o'clock in the morning, the sun was a round yellow furnace in the sky – a furnace with a ring of fog around it. There was scarcely a cloud, and even the gulls were barely floating, not flying. The lake gave a lazy now-and-then lick at the shore as if too exhausted to do more. The heat eased its way into the house and sent Jane and Elizabeth and William down to the beach. They took their toast crusts to feed the ducks.

Everything on the beach seemed so normal that Jane made a determined effort to forget about her fears and forebodings. *Wasn't it enough*, she argued with herself, *to have all that business about the doll, without me thinking we have ghosts in Aunt Alice's house? I'm getting worse than Elizabeth.*

But just as they arrived back at their own garden, Patrick came charging out of the coach house, bellowing as he came, "Where are those twins? Wait till I get my hands on them. Just wait." He saw them and thundered toward them.

"Shall we run?" whispered Elizabeth.

"Too late." Jane stood and faced Patrick.

"What do you mean going into my stuff like that?" he roared. "What do you want in there, anyhow? What have I got in there that you have to go and turn everything upside down? You kids make me so mad!" His face went dark red. His brown hair stood up in tufts where he had pushed his hands through it. His khaki pants were dirty where Horse had climbed over them with wet, muddy feet and he hadn't any shirt or shoes on. He really looked funny, and Elizabeth started to giggle.

"Don't you laugh, you little misery!" Patrick grabbed her long pony tail and pulled. In doing so he dropped something from his hand. Jane bent down and picked it up.

"What's this?" she asked, paying no attention to Patrick's anger. Elizabeth drew back out of his arm's range, rubbing her head.

"What's that," he began to roar all over again. "What do you mean, what's that? You should know. You left it there. Who else around here has bracelets and doodads and things like that?"

Jane looked closely at it. It was a bracelet made of links. Dirt and age had encrusted them, turned the metal quite green, and completely obscured their design.

"It isn't ours," Jane said flatly.

"Don't tell me that garbage," said Patrick. "Gar-bage," he said again, this time more controlled but sharp and distinct. "GAR-BAGE," he said once more and turned and marched, hands in his pockets, back to the coach house. "And," he turned back to the twins, "don't go near my stuff again. I'll skin you if I find you near that coach house."

Elizabeth looked at Jane. Jane was decidedly pale.

"What's wrong? It isn't like you to let Pat get you down."

"I don't know," Jane answered slowly. "Pat didn't bother me. He's just a steam engine." She giggled unexpectedly. "He runs down like William's windup car, doesn't he?"

Elizabeth laughed but she knew something was bothering Jane. Jane had been so silent ever since yesterday afternoon, off in a dream or something, paying no attention to her, not wanting to talk about the doll – or anything else for that matter. And now she seemed really worried. She watched Jane twist the funny old bracelet from the coach house round and round on her wrist.

"Let's see the bracelet," she said. Jane held out her arm without taking the bracelet off. "Wonder where it came from?" Elizabeth asked. "It's a funny color, isn't it?"

Jane didn't answer directly. She told about the imprisonment in the attic; about seeing the flower-patterned bedroom ("I guess that's why you saw it"); about the eyes that watched and her great fear and fight to get away ("And you know, I just remembered. That window was tight shut. The one Aunt Alice had to close that day we first came."); she told about Horse's barking in the night and Marble standing guard. She told what she had figured out about the ghosts. "And now," she finished, trying to control the worry in her voice, "this." She held up her arm with the bracelet on it.

"There," said Elizabeth abruptly, getting up and starting toward the house, "someone's trying to get our doll. I told you someone was and this proves it. All those times it was missing. They weren't accidents," she stopped and turned, her hands on her hips, "and I bet it wasn't Porridge who took it that time either."

"Ghosts."

"I don't know about that, but someone has been sneaking around here. And I'll tell you something: from now on we're just going to have to watch Amelia all the time. I think she's valuable." And away she went to get the doll.

From then on Elizabeth didn't let Amelia out of her sight. The stiff little painted face stuck out of pockets, grocery bags, swimming towels – everywhere Elizabeth went. The boys began to make jokes and Jane's friend Polly, from down the street, came especially one day to ask Jane if there was something wrong with her sister.

Jane wasn't one bit sure about Elizabeth's explanation of someone trying to get the doll. She really was afraid they'd brought ghosts to Aunt Alice's house. She asked Joe what ghosts were like and how you knew if you had them. He told her a long story about a ghost that haunted an island castle because he'd killed somebody. "It was neat. This ghost went around howling and shrieking and yelling 'peace to my soul, peace to my soul,' until the family all said he was forgiven and then he fell off a cliff into the sea with an earsplitting moan and was never heard again." Jane didn't think the story helped much, but it made her laugh listening to Joe shriek "peace to my soul" and that made her feel better.

And, feeling better, Jane began to organize in earnest. She made Elizabeth spend a whole day and a half sitting in the tower – in the heat – going over the things that had happened, the dreams and the strange feelings, the things they had done, arranging and rearranging the list to try to find some new bit of information from it.

It all seemed to boil down to the fact that they had an antique doll whose name they both knew was Amelia ("and that could be because we're twins," Jane felt obliged to remark. Elizabeth said "Twins, twins."). They had the dreams. Jane had had a scare. And there were the roses.

"Roses," cried Elizabeth, leaping dramatically onto her bed. "I know roses. Twin roses in fact. Ha! Ha!"

Jane didn't laugh.

The scare in the attic, they decided regretfully, might have had more to do with Willy Wallet and the attic being such a gloomy place than with their doll and its house.

And so it went: doll, house, Hester, roses; house, doll, roses, Hester; Hester, house, roses, doll. No more sense than ever. They were both beginning to hate the sight of the bedraggled little doll. And both were enormously relieved when, after a day and a half of this kind of concentration, their mother informed Elizabeth it was dentist day.

Jane went along downtown but she didn't go into the dentist. She window-shopped all the way down to King Street looking at the cameras and baseballs, trying to forget the worrisome feeling that hung over her. She bought an ice cream cone in a drug store and stopped to look at candies in a little shop just in from the corner of King and Yonge Streets. The window was full of irresistible pink and white candies in beautiful glass jars and cakes displayed on fluted platters.

Deciding to buy something to take home, she put her foot on the step up to the old-fashioned glass door and saw herself. The reflection was broken by the strips of wood that crisscrossed each other holding together the small squares of glass, but she could see it clearly – the long blue dress, the bonnet, the shawl. Beyond that a street where horses and carriages passed and ladies were dressed as she was, in long full skirts. The gentlemen wore tall hats. She pushed open the shop door and found herself in her red and white striped dress, her white socks and summer sandals, just inside a men's barber shop. Hastily she drew back onto the sidewalk – a sidewalk full of rushing people dressed in ordinary everyday clothes and beside it a street where cars whizzed back and forth.

There it was again, like the dreams, like the attic, pulling her away from herself.

"It's really awful," she told Elizabeth when they got home. It was after supper in their favorite place under the cherry tree in the back garden.

"I see things and then I don't see things. I remember things and then I don't remember them – things I've never seen before." She rubbed her head, jumped up, and began to walk around the garden, stopping to pull a leaf off the lilac, walking on, pulling a leaf off the cherry tree, then round again.

"It's sort of like having my memory and someone else's too. As though I'd borrowed the someone else's memory – only the one I borrowed isn't very good. I suppose it all sounds stupid, it . . ."

"It's as though the borrowed one had spaces in it and patches, like remembering a song only not remembering all of it," Elizabeth said.

"Who's is it?" Jane stopped her walking and faced her sister.

"Maybe," said Elizabeth, "it's Amelia looking for something."

"I don't see how a doll could have a memory."

"I don't either really," Elizabeth agreed, "but I don't see who else's it could be. Hester's?"

"Hester's?" Jane was appalled. "Not Hester's."

"Why not?"

"I don't know – yes I do. I don't like Hester and I like this memory – it . . . it fits."

Elizabeth started to laugh, but she stopped as what Jane had said sank in. "You're right," she said, surprised. "It does fit. Only, what you said before is true too. It isn't all there."

"I know," Jane began her walking again, "and I'd sure like to know whose memory it is that makes me see the things I see. I saw Yonge Street, I'm sure it was Yonge Street, although now I think of it I don't know why, with horses and carriages and people in olden times clothes . . ."

"Like Hester's clothes, and Amelia's clothes," Elizabeth interrupted.

"Yes, and I've seen sailing ships out on the lake – more than just the one – and that's something else. I think that the sailing ship we saw from our window belongs to that other memory."

"I think so too," put in Elizabeth.

"I've seen houses, insides and outs, that I've never been in at all and all sorts of funny things. I thought maybe it was dreaming from all those old books, but I don't think so any more."

"I'm sure it isn't, because, Jane, we didn't have them before we had the doll."

"Yes."

Elizabeth told Jane now about seeing the field and the dirt road that day by the streetcar stop.

"You know," she said, "how it always looks in the dreams, sort of double exposed. It was out in the country. The fence was the same and the big building behind it, but the rest was a dirt road and people, kids I mean, in olden times clothes. I think you were there too . . ." Her voice trailed off, trying to remember. "Anyways – what I think is, when we find that house and take Amelia back there, the dreams'll disappear. She wants that house and we have to find it for her."

"I hope so, oh I hope so," Jane cried passionately. "I suppose you're right because certainly all the things I've seen – or most of them anyway," she amended, "have the doll in them. But if it all has to do with the doll and the house and Hester," she shivered again, "then that feeling I have must have something to do with them too – and if it has," she paused and took a shaky breath, "then we'd better find it soon because I'm absolutely positive something truly dreadful is going to happen."

11

Aunt Alice Again – And a Brooch

Elizabeth sat very still. A leaf, loosened by Jane's nervous pulling, fell off the cherry tree. A squirrel dropped an acorn off the roof of the house and it bounced and rolled on the stone walk below. Elizabeth had never seen Jane so upset, not the time the kitten had been hit by a car, not the time she had nearly drowned in Margot Harper's swimming pool, not even this spring when Willy Wallet hadn't let her on the baseball team. Elizabeth made up her mind to take charge.

"Look," she said decisively, "I've been thinking and I think you were wrong. It isn't like a detective mystery. This whole thing is like one of those awful scavenger hunts – you know, where you get a clue and you have to follow it to find the next one. If you find the wrong one – like the third one second or something, it's no good, you have to go back and find the second one or you never get to what it is you're really looking for – and you don't know what *that* is till you get there."

Jane nodded. Elizabeth continued, "Well, I think this doll thing is like that. Maybe it isn't the house we're looking for at all. Maybe that's just a clue."

Jane's eyes widened with interest. "Yes," she said eagerly, "and maybe Hester's just a clue and . . ." her face fell, "but how will we know if we have the clues in the right order?"

"I think we'll just know," Elizabeth said positively. "We'll just feel if they're right. I mean if, instead of paying no attention to all the things we see and just keep looking for the house, we stop and try different things, I'm sure we'll find it – whatever it is. Anyway I'm going to make a new list."

Jane began to laugh. She laughed so hard she had to hold the branch she had perched herself on for fear of falling off. "You know what?" she said finally when she could catch her breath.

"What?"

"You sound like me and I sound like you. I have all the wild dreams and you have all the organizing schemes."

"That rhymes," they giggled. Jane felt better again. There was a plan now to work on.

"Now," said Elizabeth, "listen. First we found the doll, that's number one. Clue number two: we saw the dream house – and remember when we didn't pay any attention to it we saw it again, so that must be right. Then three: we started to hunt for the house . . ."

"And we hunted and hunted and hunted," sighed Jane.

"Yes, and we didn't find it so maybe that clue is for later."

"Well, what should we be looking for – Hester?"

"Maybe."

"Now, Elizabeth," Jane was sounding more like Jane now, and Elizabeth like Elizabeth. "You can't look for someone who lived 150 years ago or more. You just can't."

"Well, maybe we should look some more in the museum for her clothes or her brooch – I wonder what happened to her brooch after she – I suppose she grew up and died and everything."

"I suppose so."

"I never thought about that brooch. You see," Elizabeth was triumphant, "there's a whole new thing to think about. Maybe I should go upstairs and think."

"No thank you for thinking," Jane said hastily, "let's try another clue. What about the doll? Maybe we should concentrate more on Amelia." She got down from her cherry tree branch and picked Amelia up from Elizabeth's lap. "You know," she said, "we could fix up the doll, paint her face and make new clothes for her, just like the ones in the dreams – or the memories – or whatever they are."

"Yes!" Elizabeth jumped up. She didn't tell Jane she'd already tried the dressmaking. "Why don't we do that. Maybe she'll remember better if we do. That's a marvelous idea. Good for you. What'll we do first?"

Jane thought. "I think we should ask Mama," she said. "After all, she knows all about sewing and everything."

Elizabeth was doubtful about asking Mama.

"We don't have to say why," Jane argued, "we can just say we want to fix the doll up and we've been reading in books to see what she should look like."

"Well . . . , all right, we'll do it."

Their mother thought they had a fine idea. She was stuffing clothes into the clothes dryer in the basement when they found her, so they had to wait while she wrestled with the heavy sheets before she would come upstairs to look at the doll. When she did she told them the painting part was a little beyond her. "But why don't you take it to Aunt Alice," she suggested. "There she is, stuck in her apartment with her mending hip. She can't do as much of her tapestry as she'd like because the doctor said it's too heavy for her just now. I'll bet she'd be pleased as punch to help you. And she knows so much about this sort of thing too – much more than I do." Without waiting for them to say a word, Mama went to phone Aunt Alice.

"And you can take William," she added, as she dialed the number. "I've been wanting to get down to some of my own work for days, and he's bored and could use a good visit with Aunt Alice."

Aunt Alice was phoned and declared herself delighted to help the twins with their project.

"Come on, nuisance," said Jane to William and off they went, the three of them and the little doll, its face, as always, stiff with its half-painted smile and unaware of the trouble it was causing.

When they knocked at Aunt Alice's apartment door, it was opened to them by a man they had never seen before, a short, round man with no hair. "Ah," he said, smiling benignly at them, "good afternoon and have you brought a valuable historical document for us to see today?"

They thought at first they must be in the wrong place, but Aunt Alice's voice from inside, bidding them to "Come in, come in," assured them they hadn't.

"They've brought their doll," said William.

"Their doll, eh?" said the man. "Well, well." He led them through the tiny hall into Aunt Alice's big, sunny living room.

"Glad to see you. Let's see your doll, where'd you get it? . . . ah, remember now, same doll you showed me before. Glad to help. Come here Martin."

The round man obeyed as quickly and without any more question than Elizabeth had. He bent over Amelia to look closely at her.

"By George!" he said, starting with surprise. "By George! Where on earth did you get that?"

"From the Dolls Mended," said Elizabeth. "We bought it."

"Must have cost a pretty penny," he said.

"We paid two dollars and fifty-five cents," said Jane. "I guess it wasn't too much," she added, not being sure, in this case, how much too much would be.

"Too much? Why on earth would an antique dealer sell a doll like this for two dollars and fifty-five cents? Are you sure?"

Jane was still not sure whether two dollars and fifty-five cents was too much or too little. "I'm sure," she said.

"That's right," Elizabeth put in, "two fifty-five, that's how much we had and that's how much she said we had to pay."

"Well, by George, well," he said, "isn't that extraordinary. This is a very fine doll."

"Mr. Hedley works at the Royal Ontario Museum," Aunt Alice interrupted him.

"Oh," said William, nodding his head up and down, "he's the museum man. He read the blue book we sent of Papa's."

And then they all began to laugh and talk about the house moving. While Miss Weller, the housekeeper who was helping Aunt Alice until her hip was healed, got tea for them, they talked, admired the view of the city from Aunt Alice's window, and politely answered the questions Mr. Hedley was asking them about their doll.

"Yes," he said, "I know that little shop, run by an elderly woman whose name, I believe, is Miss Cloud or Miss Sky or something. I can't quite understand why she would sell you the doll for such a small amount (*Oh*, thought Jane and Elizabeth, *we paid too little*). It's quite expertly carved and really, not in too bad condition. It might be as old as 1800." He turned Amelia over and over in his hand, whistling under his breath as he thought.

"No," Elizabeth blurted out without thinking, "it's not that old."

"You mean because of its dress?" asked Mr. Hedley.

"No, because the book says the house it lived in wasn't built before 1840."

Both Aunt Alice and Mr. Hedley looked at her in great surprise. Jane looked peeved. Elizabeth wished she hadn't said anything.

"Well," she amended hastily, "we were interested and we looked up dolls and houses and things and the book said about the dress, I guess I mean, and we looked it up in the library about that kind of dress and that's what it said," she finished weakly, not daring to look at Jane at all.

"Very enterprising," Mr. Hedley said smiling vaguely, not quite understanding what Elizabeth was talking about. Aunt Alice, who was always aware when wool was being pulled over her eyes, looked at Elizabeth with one eyebrow raised. Elizabeth blushed.

William, who had apparently been totally engrossed with the cat at the foot of Aunt Alice's chair, looked up and said, "It has something to do with Hester. She lived in a red brick house with Amelia . . ."

"William," said Jane, her face red and stormy, "shut up. Just shut up!"

Mr. Hedley raised his eyebrow in alarm. Aunt Alice asked questions.

"Who is Amelia? And who is Hester?"

"Oh, just a made-up person, both of them are made-up people. It was all make-believe," Jane said quickly.

"No, it wasn't," asserted William. "You went all over the place looking for her house and . . ."

"Well, it was just pretend," Jane was trying very hard not to sound angry.

"Who is Hester?" Aunt Alice directed her question this time, and her piercing gaze, toward William.

"I don't know," answered William, "but she's somebody Jane 'n' Liza don't like."

Aunt Alice changed direction and looked from Jane to Elizabeth. It was obvious she meant to know what it was all about.

Elizabeth began to tell, reluctantly at first, but as she went on she was glad to tell the whole thing to someone other than Jane, someone who might help them find a clue. Jane was glad too. Any bits of the story Elizabeth neglected she put in, until, piece by piece, the whole tale was told – the doll, the house, Hester, Hester's brooch – everything. Miss Weller came in, unnoticed, with tea.

"And," Elizabeth said with a pleading gesture of her hands, "we don't know what to do next. The only two things so far that are at all the same are the roses on the house and the roses on the box. The rest doesn't make sense at all." She explained then her theory about a scavenger hunt and how they hoped, by restoring the doll, to find the next clue. She hoped desperately Aunt Alice wouldn't laugh.

Aunt Alice didn't laugh. She sat deep in her chair pushing her hands open and shut, open and shut against each other while she thought. It wasn't that she truly believed the doll had a memory and was sending the twins on a hunt for a long ago house. But she did believe that the world was full of things that didn't appear to make sense.

Mr. Hedley didn't laugh either. He nodded his head and thought.

"Aunt Alice has a brooch like that," said William, looking up again from his spot on the rug.

The answer he got was four blank stares. Finally Aunt Alice put down the teapot she had been busy with and said, with a brilliant smile, "You're right William, I do have a brooch like that. But how on earth did you know that?"

"You had it on when you came to see us in the old house."

"The old house?"

"Before we came to your house."

Suddenly everyone (except Mr. Hedley, of course,) remembered the day, months ago now, when Aunt Alice had come to visit them in Spring View Acres.

"My goodness," said Aunt Alice, "what a memory you have."

"When William grows up," said Jane sourly, "he's going to be an encyclopedia."

"Can we see the brooch?" Elizabeth asked eagerly.

"It's in the jewel box. Top drawer of my dresser in the bedroom, Elizabeth. We'll all have a look. Give you a good idea what you're looking for."

"Oh, we have a close idea," said Jane, a bit grimly.

Elizabeth was gone such a long time that Aunt Alice sent Jane after her. Jane found her sister standing in front of the high old dresser looking at something in her hands. Her face was the color of the gray wall behind it.

"I know it sounds crazy," she said, turning and holding the brooch out for Jane to see, "but this is Hester's brooch."

12

Elizabeth Makes Up Her Mind

Aunt Alice plainly didn't believe the twins when they said the brooch was the brooch in their dreams. If there had been something about their story that had caught her attention when they had first told it, it was easy to see that she now felt the way Joe had about the sick basket dream – it was just one of those twin things.

All the same, she gave them the brooch. "Not my style," she said as she put it into Elizabeth's hand. "Remember it was my mother's, your great-grandmother's. So take good care of it. No matter whose it was before that," she added and the twins couldn't help noticing that her eyes twinkled when she said it.

Mr. Hedley, like Aunt Alice, wasn't too interested in the brooch. But he was interested in the doll.

"I shall enquire for you," he offered, "from Miss Air or Miss Sky or whatever her name is at the antique shop, then from the specialists in dolls at the museum – I shall have to have the doll, of course, but you won't mind that, will you?" He turned a comfortable smile on the twins and Elizabeth said, "No, you can have it if we can have it right back."

"You can have it, Martin," said Aunt Alice, biting off a thread from sewing she had begun, "when its face and its clothes are done. You leave it here a while. I want to work on it . . ."

"But Alice," Mr. Hedley was outraged, "I must have it unchanged, before it is restored. Don't you see . . ."

"But we really have to take it home," said Jane picking it up from Aunt Alice's lap and holding it firmly.

Elizabeth looked at her sister in astonishment. What was Jane thinking about. Here was Aunt Alice ready to help them fix Amelia. Here was Mr. Hedley dying to take her to the museum and find out what he could about her, maybe solve the whole mystery. What did Jane mean?

"I'll have to have the doll in order to find out anything. You can trust me," he said gently. "I'll be most careful of it, most careful."

Jane knew he would. She liked Mr. Hedley. "It . . . it's not that," she said stammering a little.

"What's the matter with you," hissed Elizabeth. Jane wished she knew. She felt she had to have the doll with her. She didn't know why.

They tried to talk her out of it, but Jane wouldn't budge. (Aunt Alice wondered afterward why it was the twins' mother had told her, "You'll get on with Jane, she's like you, practical."). Finally they gave up.

"If you should change your mind," said Mr. Hedley as they were leaving, "you will get in touch with me, won't you?" Jane assured him they would, but it was Elizabeth who put his address and phone number in the pocket of her dress.

Elizabeth was getting cross. It was so hot – so heavy hot – the doll dreams were getting worse, so bad she was tired of them and a little frightened. For some reason, which she did not understand, she did not have the same feeling of real dread that Jane had. But she was worried and anxious to have the problem solved.

"Why," she asked as they walked down Hayberry Street, "won't you let Mr. Hedley have the doll?" It was the fifth time she had asked the question since they had left Aunt Alice's apartment. The answer she got was still the same – a shrug.

"But, Jane, maybe he can find the next clue. We can't do anything without that. Whatever's going to happen is just going to go right ahead and happen if we don't do something. We'll get so mixed up with that other memory we'll go plain crazy. You sure are funny!" She kicked out at a pebble that was lying loose in the street. "First you want lists and organizing and action. Now, when we get some help you won't have anything to do with it."

"I know," said Jane miserably, "I know but I can't help it. Run along William." William was looking from one twin to the other as though he were watching a tennis game.

"Yes, do," agreed Elizabeth. "You're the worst, nosy boy . . ."

"I found the brooch," said William.

"Yes, you did," Jane leaned down suddenly and gave him a tight hug. "You found the next clue William. You've been a very great help and we thank you."

Completely taken aback by the unexpected approval, William did what he always did when he was embarrassed. He began to make car motor noises, louder and louder and when he thought they were loud enough, he took off down the street toward home running his motor at top speed all the way.

"He did find the next clue, even if we don't want it," Jane said when William had rounded the corner of Sabiston Court.

"I guess so. I don't want it, that's true. But, like it or not, I guess you're right. It's our next clue."

That night was a series of nightmares for both of them, and morning brought no comfort. Jane woke quickly in the early heat with Hester's face fading away from the light. Elizabeth, seeing the look on Jane's face, dragged her down to the beach. She tried once more to convince Jane to let Aunt Alice and Mr. Hedley have the doll. It was no use.

Elizabeth had never felt so frustrated. She understood Jane's mood so well. Hadn't she often been in black moods, moods Jane had never had any patience with? She knew now how Jane must have felt about them.

"Let's go home," she said with resignation. And they left the ducks to eat somebody else's toast crusts.

Their mother, seeing them come up through the garden as she was making breakfast, said to their father, "I'm worried about Jane."

"Why?"

"Well, she seems so pale and jumpy. Not a bit like Jane. And another thing," she handed Papa a piece of toast, "have you ever seen Jane so wrapped up in a doll?"

Mr. Hubbard admitted he hadn't.

"Even when the twins were tiny," Mama said, "they, especially Jane, seldom looked at dolls, and now neither one of them can leave that antique alone for a single minute."

"They've developed an interest in history and antiques. They're growing up." Papa looked pleased.

"Maybe," said Mama. "But I think there's something strange about it and I don't like it. I'm going to try . . . Hello," she said as the twins came in the door. "Fried or scrambled?" and whatever it was Mama intended to say about the twins' strange behavior never got said. She put them to work that morning – to try to work out of the twins whatever it was that bothered them.

Obediently they swept and dusted, but the things that happened only made them more frantic. Jane's heavy black mood clung to her tighter and tighter as the morning progressed. She couldn't help herself. And the heat of the last week seemed, this morning, to be gathered altogether in one lump, settling over their edge of the city. The sun was barely visible through the heat haze, but its effect was in no way diminished. It was too hot to move. But Jane tried. As she worked things got worse.

She was sweeping out the fireplace in the dining room when she heard a voice behind her say, "Sweep the corners, Nan, it's bread day," and thought she saw the edge of a long green dress disappear into the kitchen. But when she went into the kitchen there was only Mama there, not making bread but washing dishes. She gritted her teeth, finished her sweeping, and went into the garden to weed around Aunt Alice's kitchen vegetable patch.

Someone rushed past her, laughing, and whispered, "Whist! I'm for the barn. Here she comes." Footsteps retreated in haste down the stone walk and when she looked up there was Hester coming toward her. She dropped the trowel from her perspiring hand and forced her shaking legs to stand. Hester vanished. Jane leaned weakly against the side of the house, pushing her wet hair from her hot forehead. She was shaking. *I'm going to be like old Mrs. Van der Zande*, she thought, *poor old Mrs. Van der Zande who could never remember if she was Mrs. Van der Zande or Mary Queen of Scots about to have her head cut off.* She tried to smile at the idea, but it wasn't funny and her lips trembled at the attempt.

Leaving her trowel where she had dropped it, she walked toward the house.

Elizabeth watched her from behind the living room curtain. She was a bit shaken herself – and for the same reason. A few minutes earlier she had been cleaning the dining room windows when she heard someone singing. It had sounded like Jane, and since the song was "Barbara Allen," a song Jane very often sang, she hadn't thought anything of it at all. In fact she had even hummed along with it a way. The song had stopped and a voice, not Jane's, had said, "If they come you'll stay this time," and then quite sternly, "do you hear, Liss?"

She had felt an answer come to her own lips when Mama had called from the next room, "Elizabeth, Aunt Alice is on the phone and wants to know how high your doll is." Elizabeth nearly cried. She had been so near something, she was sure she had, so near understanding something terribly important. She tried to get back into the memory but without success. It was at that point she saw Jane outside, leaning against the stone wall of the house. She put down the window spray and made up her mind. She marched out of the house.

"Why don't you go for a swim?" she asked Jane. "Maybe you'll feel better." Jane looked at her from frightened eyes.

"Come on, go get your suit, I'll finish the weeding." Jane told Elizabeth about Hester. "Never mind," said Elizabeth. "I'll take a chance. You go on."

Relieved to have moral support, Jane agreed. Elizabeth watched her go into the house and waved her away a few minutes later when she came back out again on her way to the lake. As soon as she was out of sight, Elizabeth dropped the trowel and, disregarding the heat, raced into the house and up to the tower bedroom. She grabbed the paper with Mr. Hedley's address and phone number from the pocket of the dress she had worn the day before. She dashed back downstairs and phoned the number, praying with every turn of the black dial that he would answer her call. He did. Would he be in that afternoon, Elizabeth asked, and could she bring the doll to him? He would and would be delighted.

Quickly telling Mama where she was going, Elizabeth ran back up the stairs, changed her clothes, and took the doll from its hiding place.

"There," she said, smoothing down its tattered clothes, "we'll know now, we'll find out for you, you'll see." She put Amelia in her box and left the house, feeling only a twinge of guilt at playing this trick on her sister.

"She'll be all right, though," Elizabeth told herself. "After all, the whole family's there. And we have to find out, we just have to."

13

Hester

Elizabeth hadn't been gone ten minutes when Papa emerged from his study, came into the back garden, and flopped down on the grass. Mama followed him minutes later with two glasses of iced coffee.

"It's too hot to breathe. This is a devil's day, a real devil's day. I move we all go to the show," Papa said between sipping his coffee and mopping his forehead.

"What's playing?" asked Mama. But Papa said he didn't care as long as the movie theater had air-conditioning.

They found Joe lying on his bed listening to the radio, eagerly keeping track of the weather reports.

"Boy," he said, "it hasn't been this hot in July since 1838. Wow!"

Pat was in the coach house and William was retrieved from the basement, where he had made an underground car park.

"Where are the twins?" asked Papa, and Mama, thinking they had both gone to see Mr. Hedley, told him so.

"Very well, leave them a note saying we prefer the cool of – what is it we're going to see?"

"*Captain Belmish Returns*," said Joe gleefully. Papa gulped, "Captain Belmish returns to the heat of Number Five Sabiston Court. Tell them if they care to come and meet us at the restaurant across the street from the theater – it is air-conditioned, isn't it Patrick?"

Joe, who always knew these things, said it was and had neat french fries besides. Mama wrote the note, put it on the kitchen table, and they left.

And so, when Jane came up from her swim not in the least soothed, she found silence. Marble had sought relief from the heat under the kitchen window. Horse was in his favorite spot under the lilac bush. No leaf stirred on the cherry tree and the heat hung heavy over everything.

Inside, the house was empty and still. She found the note on the kitchen table and went upstairs to change. In the mood she was in, the silence upstairs seemed ominous. No breeze disturbed the curtains at her window. Only the floor creaked as she walked across it. The feeling of being watched she had had that day in the attic came back now. Quickly, nervously, she put on her red shorts and top. Barefooted, she went back downstairs and out of the house. She couldn't stay in it. It terrified her. She hated Elizabeth for going off to the movies and leaving her like this. When she saw Horse it made her feel better.

Bolstered by his presence she said out loud (to whom? to the watching eyes?), "I'll ignore the whole thing, the way Liza does. I'll just pay no attention," and she turned her back to the house and tried to rouse Horse to play a game. He only opened one eye, looked at her, and closed it.

After a few minutes she couldn't bear not looking at the house – in case someone was there ready to come out at her. She lectured herself again, "Don't be foolish," she said sternly, "why should you ignore it. Just go right in there. Get yourself some lemonade and a book or something." And, obeying her own orders, she did that walking carefully into the kitchen whistling "Barbara Allen" under her breath, and then into Papa's study whistling a little more loudly, and pounced on the first book that came to hand – the one open on Papa's desk. It was *City on the Lake: Being a Brief History of Toronto 1793-1864*, by William Sabiston.

"Why didn't we think of this," she said to herself, "when we were looking for books? Maybe Great-Great-Uncle has something in his book we can use." Feeling a trifle guilty about taking it from Papa's desk, she shoved it under her arm and walked with great speed back to the garden. There she settled herself – not too far from Horse – to try to read the book and drink her lemonade.

"When my grandfather, Patrick Sabiston, set sail from far off England," she read, "accompanied by his wife, his twin daughters and his two sons, for this untrammelled wilderness by the lake, this shining big sea water as it was then called by the native Indians who had lived savage by its shore for so many centuries, he little dreamed how successful would be his venture, or what triumphs and griefs there were in store for him and his family. Muddy little York (for our now fair and burgeoning city was then known all over the world as 'muddy little York,' a town to be ridiculed and scorned by visitors from older cities on the other side of the great ocean) was then in . . ."

Jane's attention slid off Great-Great-Uncle's endless and tedious sentences. The book was no help. The fear she was trying so hard to keep down rose again in her throat.

"Oh Horse," she whispered, rolling over and nuzzling him closely, "I'm so glad you've grown so nice and big." She sat up and forced her attention back to the book, her eyes touching bits of sentences up and down the pages. It didn't seem to be a history of Toronto as much as of the Sabiston family and their house. "Houses," she muttered, "I know all about them," and went skipping through, "homestead by the lake . . . log house . . . later additions obscured the original shape . . . tower my father appended to the northwest corner, fine view of the lake and the cherry tree garden below . . ." Jane put down the book in surprise.

"Why, he means this house." She looked at the house, curiosity for the moment getting the better of fear. "I wonder what it looked like?" Then it occurred to her, "I suppose it looked like all those other houses we've been looking at. When was it built first, anyway?" She picked up the book and leafed quickly back through it. "Here it is,

'The first log house was constructed in 1833 to be replaced in two years by a more substantial brick structure of the kind fashionable at that time.'"

"Well I know what that was," said Jane, and began trying to puzzle out the old house inside the shape of the new.

"There's the peak, just below the tower over our door," she murmured holding up her forefinger and tracing its outline as though she were drawing a sketch. "There's the roof line, no trim though – yes, it must be under the ivy."

The outline of the little house was beginning to show itself to her, like the cat or the teacup in the pictures where it says, "find the hidden whatever it is."

"Then Porridge's pigeon hole and that other one across from it must be part of the decoration," she said staring at the back of the house in deep concentration. Suddenly, it was all there, the complete outline of the "substantial brick structure." She could see the whole thing, hidden though it was by so many years of entwining ivy – a small, red brick house with a low door, a window above, and, at either side of the door, white wood lace trim twirling and curving to make two circular designs near the second floor gable peak. "Roses," said Jane in a dry whisper, "not pigeon holes, roses – all the time. It was here, all the time it was here – in Aunt Alice's house – our house, Amelia's house, Hester's house."

She jumped to her feet, the big house faded and the little one was left, its brick new and bright red, its ivy a thin runner of baby green leaves along one side, its white wood trim freshly painted with the two roses clearly visible over the low door. Not the kitchen door of Aunt Alice's house, but the front door of the other one, its stone step in front of it and the little yellow and white butter and eggs flowers growing around it and in its cracks. Not Hester's house, her house. She was still standing there beside the cherry tree, not old and gnarled now, but small and young and straight. And the water was visible out of the edge of her eye – not a pond or creek as Elizabeth had assumed, but the whole of Lake Ontario – still and pewter gray under the sultry sky, the same sky, the same hot heat there had been for days. She was still Jane standing there, but now she was the other person too. She looked down at herself and saw she was wearing a long dress, blue, the dress from the sick basket dream, from the candy store on King Street. She had no shoes on.

The other person likes barefoot too, she thought, wriggling her toes in the grass, and was glad. Her hair was the same as it had always been, two long brown braids, hot and sticky on her head, and she was surprised to see that she still wore the bracelet Pat had found in the coach house.

"Oh no, it's not the same," she said, and held her wrist up to see, but it was the same, only new, so new you could see the roses.

"Roses," she said, shaking her head, "roses again. Why didn't we see that, roses, painted red and white, rose red and snow white . . ."

Nervously she smoothed down the unfamiliar long skirt. The other's memory began to intrude and she heard herself say, "I'm coming," and felt the other's irritation.

"Oh Hester, don't be so impatient," she heard herself say, almost as though it were someone else saying it – but not quite.

And then the fear that was her own came rushing back. The house faded a little, the big house reappeared as if in a double exposed photograph.

"I won't go in there," she cried, "I won't go!" but felt herself, willy-nilly, with the touch of her long skirt against the grass, walking toward the house. It was like being a bone, torn between two dogs.

"Elizabeth," called Jane, "Liza, please come home!" A face appeared at the upstairs window, the big house faded once more, the feet under the long skirt continued toward the house.

From under the lilac bush, Horse began to whine. "Oh Horse," cried Jane in a last frantic plea, "please come with me!" But Horse, his fur standing up in a ridge along his spine, backed further under the bush, watching her unhappily from under his tangled white hair.

"I'm coming, Hester," she called to the upstairs window, "I'm coming."

❀ 14 ❀

Melissa

It was at this point that Elizabeth, just getting on the subway to take her to Mr. Hedley's Avenue Road apartment, stopped short, felt Jane's frantic plea for help, turned around, and took the next streetcar back. All the way into town she had felt uneasy. She had explained it to herself by saying it was because she felt guilty taking the doll to Mr. Hedley without Jane's permission, but suddenly she knew it wasn't and she was scared. And then she saw it too. Sitting at the back of the streetcar, surrounded by noisy, chattering people, the picture of their house – Aunt Alice's house – leapt into her mind and over it, the same way Jane had seen it, like a double exposed photograph, the little house of their dream. Its peaked roof ended just below the tower window, its white wood carved roses fitted themselves neatly over the pigeon holes of Aunt Alice's house, its front yard settled into the kitchen garden. And, just as it had happened with Jane, Aunt Alice's house faded. The dream became reality and Elizabeth was sharing completely the memory of someone who had lived in that smaller, older house.

She remembered now, not as two people, but as one, the other girl in her long blue dress. She remembered, as the other must so often have done, horror and grief. Smoke was pouring out of the upstairs window. She could feel heat – the hot sultry heat of the day and the heat of the flames from upstairs. There was a crowd of people, shouting and running, then suddenly quiet. She was trying desperately to get into the house but someone's big hands were holding her back.

"I have to go in there," she was sobbing. "You can't stop me. It's my sister in there. She'll die! You can't stop me." Then understanding without being told, understanding from the silence of the crowd outside that it was too late, she looked up and saw Hester, Hester in a pink dress with red ribbons on it, half-hidden behind her mother's fashionable wide brown skirt, Hester looking white and scared.

She screamed at Hester, she remembered it so clearly, "It's your fault, it's your fault," over and over again. "It's your fault. Oh Hester, I hate you, I hate you forever and ever! Oh Anne . . ." and then the sobs that seemed never to cease.

It was all there, the memory of that day, with the agony of its first happening, and Elizabeth Hubbard sitting on the streetcar, her fist clenched over a small wooden doll that had once belonged to that other girl – that other twin – remembered it all. And the memory was like a flood let loose over a broken dam, pouring out, carrying with it bits of memory from other days: an instant of joy with Anne in the winter snow, a trip in the cart with a new spring lamb, the misery of saying good-bye to the little house and the lake, the sailing ship on its way back to England.

But as the strength of that one tortured memory faded, so did the others, and Elizabeth was herself again. Rubbing the tears away from her cheeks, sniffing shakily and ignoring the stares of nearby passengers, she tried to sort things out. "It was twins," she said. "Twins. Why didn't we see it was twins? We should have seen that. Twin roses – two of them. That's why it was us. We should have known that. It wasn't the same memory we borrowed, not Hester's, not the doll's. Jane had one and I had one and the roses were for two . . . and it was our house, of course it was our house, not Hester's house and Hester was . . ." Elizabeth's stomach turned over. She realized who Hester was. "Hester is Jane's ghost," she cried out loud, causing the stares to become more pointed and the woman beside her to get up and move away. "It's Hester who's been doing all the things, Hester who was in the attic, Hester who . . . oh glory . . . and Jane is there." Elizabeth jumped up from her seat and got off the streetcar at the next stop – four stops before Hayberry Street.

"I'm coming," she whispered as she hurried along the street. She wished achingly that she'd paid more attention to Jane's fears. How could she have been so stupid? she wondered, she who had known from the beginning that something strange was going on, who'd said all along that there was a clue somewhere they were missing. How could she have ignored Jane's feeling about the ghost? It was all so obvious now. "I'm coming, Jane, oh please don't let it be too late."

She began to run, bumping into people as she did, past stores, houses, apartments, her breath heaving up from the bottom of her stomach, perspiration streaming down her face, sticking her hair tight to her head and wetting a dark round spot on the back of her white shirt. "I'm coming," she kept saying in uneven rhythm to her stumbling feet. And all the while, at the back of her head, was the picture of that other day and that other twin. Tears came again and mixed with the sweat on her face.

She raced down Hayberry Street in a last sprint of energy, along Sabiston Court, around the corner of the house and was staggering toward the back door when an unearthly sound from the garden stopped her cold. The hair at the back of her neck prickled and her hot skin turned cold with goose flesh. It came again. A howl, a moan, almost a scream. By will power she hadn't known she had, Elizabeth slowly turned around. Terror evaporated and she collapsed on the ground, her legs like melting jelly.

Horse, terrified by what was happening in the house and garden, had never emerged from his shelter under the lilac bush. His haunches deep under the bush, his unruly head shoved as close into the ground as he could get it, he had lain there, glaring balefully at the house.

When he saw Elizabeth rounding the corner of the house, headed in his direction, his tail began to thump in hopeful anticipation. But when he saw her stumbling right by him, not seeing him at all, he couldn't help himself. He opened his mouth and let out a yowl of pain and despair.

"Oh Horse," sighed Elizabeth through her deep, exhausted breathing, "oh, Horse," and he looked so awkward and foolish, still not willing to come out from under his bush, his tail thumping like a drum against the earth, his eyes beseeching her so mournfully, she began to laugh. And it was laughter that saved Elizabeth, gave her back her sense and reason and a kind of courage she may never have had before, and probably saved Jane's life.

She lay there a moment, her cheek against Horse's ecstatic head. "I love you, Horse," she said at last, "but if you won't come with me, I'll have to go without you," and she walked steadily to the house, through the back door and up the stairs to the old attic. The door wouldn't open.

"Jane," she called firmly through the door, "Jane, it's me, Elizabeth."

🌹 15 🌹

Anne

Inside the attic Jane heard, but dimly, as though the voice outside was the unreal dream voice and what was happening here, inside, was real. She wasn't Jane now. She hadn't been since the moment she entered the house following Hester's call. Jane was somewhere deep inside a distant, borrowed memory. She was the living memory of another girl named Anne and she was standing, not in the dreary gray attic with its clumsily repaired floor, she was in a bright bedroom with walls that had stripes of roses and green leaves freshly painted on. There was a big wooden bed, with low carved posts, a bed she shared with her sister Melissa. There was a small washstand in one corner with a new pink wash basin and ewer they had got from England for Christmas. In the other corner was a square table with a candle on it. Across from that was a blanket chest over which hung the sampler she had spent so many months working. There were white woven curtains at the window, curtains that hung limp in the excessive heat of the July day.

She was having an argument with her cousin Hester. Hester lived in Toronto, five miles away. Anne didn't like Hester, neither did Lissa, and Hester knew it. Hester scorned their house in the country, their plain homespun clothes – even their new blue dresses. Her own were always in the latest style (*as though*, thought Anne, *her fat arms were any prettier under those fat sleeves over her elbows*) and made of cloth imported from England – flowered cloth. Hester was a tale bearer and her idea of having fun when she came to visit was to tease the dog, Claverhouse, get the sheep all upset by throwing pebbles into their midst, or turn the pig loose. At least she used to do those things. Nowadays she spent more time making much of the twins' older brother William.

She laughed at the idea of farmers (although the twins had noticed she was always out and about when Halpern, the hired man, was anywhere in sight).

She liked to poke around and try on Mama's best finery too, but most of all Hester delighted in causing trouble for the twins. Mama said they had to be kind because she was their cousin. It was Anne's nature to be kind to people but she found it exceedingly difficult to be kind to Hester. She was finding it difficult now. Lissa had run off when she'd spied Hester arriving, and Anne had been doing her best to be kind and entertaining for over an hour – and it was so unbearably hot. She had listened to Hester talk about her new frock and her four fine muslin petticoats, a new shop on King Street that sold French bonnets, how elegant the Lieutenant-Governor's lady was, and other bits of what Anne considered useless conversation.

Bored, and sensing Anne was not as impressed as she thought she should be, Hester wanted to seek out Melissa. Melissa was more interested in gowns and bonnets and would be more easily impressed.

"Where is she anyhow?" demanded Hester. "Why must she be gone so long?"

Anne murmured something about Mrs. Henderson up the road, eggs, back soon, hoping Hester would be satisfied.

"It's getting dark," she said, hoping to change the subject. "Perhaps we'll have rain. Why don't we go downstairs and help with tea."

"Don't be such a goody, always wanting to be mama's helper. Be glad to get out of a job for once. You'll be a perfect farmer's wife, Anne, I declare you will."

"I like farmers," Anne said good naturedly. "Come, let's go downstairs. It's so hot."

"I'll not go looking for work. Why seek work, it finds you fast enough. But go if you like, I'm going to stay here."

Anne sighed and pushed the hot, heavy hair back from her face. She knew she had to stay with Hester. She wished Melissa would come out of hiding.

As if Hester could read Anne's mind, she said, "I'm going to hide Lissa's doll. Serve her right for not being here. Silly dolls anyway. Mama says I'm too old for dolls. You should be too. Let's just hide it."

Hester would, too. Anne knew she would, and cross though she herself was at Melissa's absence, she couldn't be so unkind. Mama had saved them the scraps from their new blue dresses and Lissa was planning an entire costume for Amelia. She knew how wild she would be if the doll were missing.

"Where is it?" asked Hester.

"Oh, Hester," said Anne, exasperated at last, "don't be so . . . so . . ."

"So what, Mistress Goody Two Shoes?" Hester struck a light in the now almost totally dark room and held it to the candle. The look on her usually sullen face was mocking. Something about it made Anne shiver.

"Anyway," Anne brightened, "if Lissa can't find her doll, she'll just use mine. So it's no use hiding hers."

Hester's face changed, grew, if possible, more unpleasant.

"I'll just take yours, then, too." She started toward the bed where Anne's little wooden doll was propped primly on the bolster.

"You with your twin dolls. You think you're so perfect, you two, with never any thought for anyone besides yourself. When I come here, and mercy knows I don't want to come, one of you runs off and the other makes pretend to be my friend. But I know how you feel. You don't like me because I'm not like you, all in love with a stupid farm or still playing with those hateful dolls. You don't need anyone else, you two, *you two*," she spat out those last words as though they were sour apples. The mockery was gone from her face. It was a face twisted with envy and hatred. The candle held stiffly in front of her, its flicker highlighting her face, Hester looked a creature of true evil. She started toward Anne.

Anne screamed. Outside it thundered, there was a white flash of lightning.

It was now that Elizabeth began pounding and shouting at the attic door from the other side. "Janie, Janie let me in! Please let me in! It's Hester in there, let me in!"

Jane's memory buried beneath the force of Anne's, began to work. But it was still Anne who cried out passionately, "Don't hate us, Hester. Why do you hate us so? We don't hate you. Honestly we don't. We can't help being two people, that's the way we were born."

"Yes you do, you two, always two of you, hating me, laughing behind my back, making up stories about me." Hester's face lost its look of evil and crumpled up in misery. The candle wavered in her hand. Outside the rain began to fall in sheets. Anne walked toward her, to comfort her unhappy cousin.

"Oh, Hester, we can't help the way we are. You see, we sort of come in two halves. You have to have us both for friends because we're like that. Please, Hester, don't cry so." Just as Anne stretched out her arms toward the sobbing Hester, Hester, consumed by her own woe, forgot she was holding the candle and let it slip.

Outside the door, her calls getting no answer, Elizabeth lost her temper. "Hester," she bellowed, "What are you doing? Come out of there. You leave my sister alone. What do you mean haunting us anyhow?" She kicked the door violently with her foot.

Where her anguished pleas had failed, Elizabeth's shouting succeeded. Jane heard. She remembered who she was – but Anne's memory went on relentlessly reliving what had happened in that room: remembering the lighted candle falling from Hester's shaking hand, remembering the sight of her own blue dress suddenly a burst of orange flame, remembering Hester running from the room. Suffocating with terror she was being inched toward the window. It was as though she was under a spell driving her back toward the low sill. She couldn't help herself. Desperately she wanted to escape the memory of those flames. She had to reach the door, to find Elizabeth. Jane began to fight. With all her will, a thousand times stronger than she had fought that other time in the attic room, Jane struggled against remembering the rest.

"Hester," yelled Elizabeth, pounding on the door. "Hester, give up. It's our turn for this house. You give it up. You're nothing anyhow! You're absolutely nothing! You're just a poltergeist, a poltergeist," she screamed, "a poltergeist!"

Jane, inches from the window sill, came back 180 years to the abandoned attic that had once been a bright flower-painted bedroom for those other twins. And, with the complete return of her own memory, the door swung open. Elizabeth stopped shouting.

Outside, the rain was pouring steadily down. Shaking and chill, Jane knew she was not finished. She spoke carefully into the blackness where Hester had stood.

"We don't hate you, Hester," she said. "They didn't hate you either, but I don't suppose," she added honestly, "they loved you either because, you know, you weren't very nice to them. But they didn't leave you out of things on purpose. We wouldn't either. It's just . . . it was just there are two of us . . . were two of them," she stopped, confused, "two of all of us, I guess. Anne said it, too, we come in two halves. We don't always like it either." Jane couldn't see but she felt tears of misery running down Hester's face.

"You can't help it, couldn't," she amended, "being the way you were," Jane sighed, "and we can't help being the way we are and if we're more the same than most people we can't help that either." She stopped, not knowing what to say next. Suddenly she remembered Joe and his silly story about ghosts haunting until they're forgiven.

"It was an accident," she said softly. "You didn't mean to set the fire. I know you didn't. It wasn't your fault. You shouldn't have run away," she scolded gently as though she were talking to a baby. "I guess you've been well and truly punished for that, though."

Elizabeth came slowly across the room to stand beside Jane. She was still clutching Great Uncle William's book she had absentmindedly picked up in the garden. "And if she hated you all her life after that," Elizabeth explained, as patiently and gently as Jane had done, and Jane knew, by "her," Elizabeth meant Melissa, "she couldn't help it. She shouldn't have been so mean, but Anne was her twin and she couldn't help it. She just couldn't." There were tears in Elizabeth's eyes now, too, and tears trickling down her cheeks.

Jane spoke again. "You were scared, I know that, but you didn't mean to do that awful thing. Please. You can go away now. It was an accident, Hester. I promise you it was an accident."

She paused for a moment, listening, waiting. Then she said, "Where did you put it, Hester?" and waited again. "After the accident, I mean," she prompted and although Hester said not a word, in a moment Jane went over to the edge of the room where the sloping roof made a deep triangle with the floor. She felt with her hand way into its corner. There was a hole just there in the floor and under it her hand felt a space and came upon the thing she was looking for. She brought it out and took it over to the window.

Dusty, faded, very dirty, its clothes almost completely eaten away by moths, the little wooden doll was in every way identical to the one Elizabeth still held tightly in her hand.

Together they turned and faced Hester's corner. Jane spoke. "If you were mean and hateful at all, Hester, it was a long time ago now and it's all been made right. I'm sure it has."

"You can rest now," said Elizabeth.

There was silence in the attic. The rain was falling softly and steadily outside. Horse was waiting by the attic door and, closing it carefully behind them, the twins went with him down the stairs.

Epilogue

In the end, it was Aunt Alice who helped the twins sort out the bits and pieces of Anne and Melissa's story – not the story, they already knew that – but the things that came later, and it took over a month to do it.

They went to her, even though they knew she didn't believe in ghosts, because they thought she might be able to tell them things about the family.

But Aunt Alice, as she always did, surprised them. She listened closely to their story, raising and lowering her eyebrows a few times, tapping her fingers against the window sill she sat by, and when they were finished she said, "Humph," and sent Miss Weller to get the old family Bible from the bookshelf.

There they were: Anne and Melissa Sabiston, born January 12, 1825, to William and Phoebe Sabiston, in Raggs Hollow, Yorkshire, England. There were others too, born to William and Phoebe: a son William, born March 2, 1818 and Patrick, born April 4, 1830.

Anne's death was entered in the Bible July 22, 1838 (the reading of which caused Aunt Alice to say, "Humph," again). Melissa wasn't in the Bible any more – but Hester was: Hester Armitage, born May 21, 1823, died June 4, 1895, and a brother, William Armitage, born June 3, 1832.

"Why," said Aunt Alice in surprise, "that was old Aunt Hissy! Died when I was five years old." She put down the book and sat, looking out the window.

"Nobody liked her, remember that, though I don't remember her much myself – always smelled of lavender, still can't stand that smell – always black dresses. She was an old maid like me."

"Oh Aunt Alice, not like you," Jane said vehemently.

"Well, she never married. Ruled our house like an old witch woman. Lived in that room we used afterward for an attic. Never liked it there, always thought she'd left bits of herself behind – or the memory of them."

Aunt Alice looked thoughtfully at the two girls sitting on the floor by her chair. "Humph," she said once more.

"How did that room ever get to be Hester's in the first place, I want to know," asked Jane.

"Well, I suppose," said Aunt Alice, frowning, "the house simply belonged to her."

"But it didn't," Elizabeth jumped up. "It wasn't her house. It was Anne's and Melissa's. She just came to visit, remember?" she turned to Jane.

"Yes," said Jane, "and besides, if it was her house why did she only live in the attic?"

"Don't know," answered Aunt Alice. "You know, you've got me curious, stirred my old memories all up, bottom ones all bubbling up to the top. Remember old Aunt Hissy, now, sitting there like an old broody hen – horrible old woman. Children," she snapped shut the big Bible decisively, "if we want to know things you'll have to be my legs."

For the next week or so Aunt Alice sent Jane and Elizabeth to the church her father's family had always gone to, to the City Hall, to the Ontario archives where old records are kept, and, on a hunch of Elizabeth's, to the sailing records of ships that sailed out of Toronto in the year 1838.

Among the old church records they found the marriage recorded of Melissa Jane Howarth to William Armitage, October 1, 1870. They couldn't decide who these two people were because they knew their Melissa's name was Sabiston, although they thought William Armitage might have been Hester's brother. The next recording was that these two people had a son, William, born on July 8, 1872.

Jane was delighted to find him there, "I guess that's the William who wrote the book." The records went on to tell that William Armitage married Margaret MacGregor and that they had children named Alice, Arthur, Patrick and twins, Julia and Jane.

"Why," said Elizabeth, "that's Aunt Alice and old Uncle Arthur and Grandma and . . ."

"Well, then Grandma was a twin, too! I've never heard her say that."

They saw why when they read that Jane's death was recorded three years after her birth.

They were thoughtful for a minute after reading this. "I guess we're just lucky," said Jane quickly and read on, bringing the family up to date as far as their mother's birth.

"We should all be in there," Jane decided – "and in the old Bible, too," said Elizabeth and they determined to ask if they could be put in.

They had to write to the National Archives in Ottawa to find what Elizabeth wanted to know. It was not in the year 1888 where she had thought it would be, but on the *Royal Lady*, sailing from Toronto harbor, May 4, 1839, the passenger list included William and Phoebe Sabiston, their son Patrick and their daughter Melissa. "William must have been old enough to stay here," said Jane.

"So," said Elizabeth softly to herself, "she went away on the ship." And she could almost remember being on the ship, clutching the little wooden doll.

The story, or at least the family history, was beginning to fill out. But before they were finished they had to wait for Aunt Alice to write and get an answer from a cousin in Yorkshire, England. The cousin, whose name was Anne (which excited the twins) wrote this:

"My dear Alice, So sorry to hear about broken hip, hope mended, don't up too soon." (How the twins giggled at this distant cousin using these same shortcuts – only more – Aunt Alice always used.) "Looked up record you asked. Herewith: great-grandmother née Melissa Sabiston married John Howarth. He died 1857, buried village churchyard. No record here. ("Oh," said the twins, disappointedly. "Now wait," Aunt Alice cautioned.) Six children recorded: Anne Elizabeth, Melissa Jane born 1850 ("Oh," cried the twins, a very different sound from the last disappointed oh, "then that's the one who married William Armitage in 1870.") William born 1852, James born 1853, Alice born 1855 died 1856." ("How sad," said Jane.)

Here Aunt Alice's voice began to get excited.

"Now," she said, "listen." Elizabeth read over her shoulder: "Anne Elizabeth m Rob't Drover of Ntgmshr (my grdfthr)."

"What on earth does all that mean?"

Aunt Alice translated: "Anne Elizabeth married Robert Drover of Nottinghamshire (my grandfather)."

"Your grandfather?" asked Jane, completely bewildered.

"No," said Aunt Alice, "hers."

"Oh."

"Wh. went to India," the letter went on in its own kind of shorthand the twins insisted was like reading one of their mother's lists of moving instructions or grocery shopping.

"Jas m Amy Armstrong also Ntgmshr (probably related) Melissa J emigrated Canada 1868."

"You see," Elizabeth sang, "you see, there she is!"

"– and must have taken mother because no burial record here. Hope have been help must fly, Anne."

"Well," said Aunt Alice when the twins said nothing, "get me the Bible."

"But what about Hester?" asked Elizabeth. "How come she lived in the house and ran it and everything?"

"Don't know," said Aunt Alice again, "but there she was. Maybe they took her in. Old maids had to live somewhere in those days. Didn't go to work. Had to accept charity."

"Then it never was her house," said Jane.

"And she had to live in it," Elizabeth added, almost to herself. "She had to live in it all that time. You know, I am sorry for Hester. I really am."

"I know," said Jane. "It must have been awful. No wonder there's still a memory of her."

"I wonder if that's what ghosts really are, memories," said Elizabeth, "leftover memories, left loose because they weren't finished. Then when someone comes along and finds them and finishes them, they disappear."

"I'm going to give her back her brooch," Jane decided. And she did. She wrapped it up in a new piece of blue cotton cloth and put it deep down in the hole where the twin doll had been hidden all those years. And, after that, they seldom talked of Hester.

They never learned, search through records and historical documents though they might, what finally happened to Melissa. There was no record of her death or burial and it made the twins sad. They felt as though Melissa had never stopped grieving. They never found out, either, how the little doll came to be in the Antiques, Dolls Mended shop.

There were many things the twins never understood about all of it but there was no doubt that it changed the way they felt and thought about each other.

It was Jane who said it.

"It's true," she said, "what I told Hester."

"You mean about being two halves of a person?"

"Yes, two halves and that's that."

"I suppose it is." Elizabeth thought for a minute. "I mean if that's the way we are I guess that's the way we are, isn't it?"

"Maybe it isn't so bad." Jane picked up the two wooden dolls from the window seat.

"We'll have to paint them both," she said, smoothing her hand over first one chipped head and then the other.

"Yes," Elizabeth smiled at Jane. Jane smiled back. A smile? two smiles? two half-smiles? They didn't care.

GENEALOGY

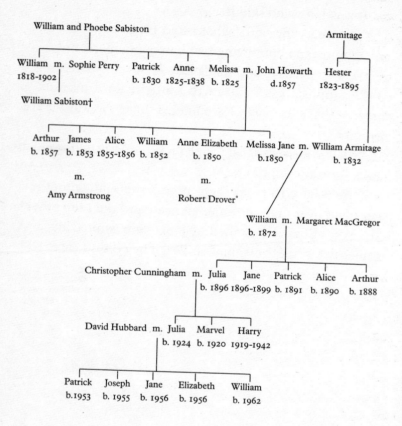

William and Phoebe Sabiston   Armitage

William m. Sophie Perry   Patrick   Anne   Melissa m. John Howarth   Hester
1818-1902   b. 1830   1825-1838   b. 1825   d.1857   1823-1895

William Sabiston†

Arthur   James   Alice   William   Anne Elizabeth   Melissa Jane m. William Armitage
b. 1857   b. 1853   1855-1856   b. 1852   b. 1850   b.1850   b. 1832

m.   m.

Amy Armstrong   Robert Drover°

William m. Margaret MacGregor
b. 1872

Christopher Cunningham m. Julia   Jane   Patrick   Alice   Arthur
                 b. 1896   1896-1899   b. 1891   b. 1890   b. 1888

David Hubbard m. Julia   Marvel   Harry
           b. 1924   b. 1920   1919-1942

Patrick   Joseph   Jane   Elizabeth   William
b.1953   b. 1955   b. 1956   b. 1956   b. 1962

† author of *City on the Lake: Being a Brief History of the City of Toronto, 1793-1861*
° grandparents of English cousin, Anne